"You don't want to be married, Jock.

"Baby or not, I am not marrying any man who doesn't love me."

Jock took a deep breath, steadying himself. "Tina, that's blackmail."

"Well, it's a strange kind of blackmail," Tina retorted. "There's a common misconception that love comes before marriage. I might love you, Jock Blaxton, but there is no way on this earth I'm marrying you if you don't love me right back."

Marion Lennox has had a variety of careers—medical receptionist, computer programmer and teacher. Married, with two children, she now lives in rural Victoria, Australia. Her wish for an occupation that would allow her to remain at home with her children and her dog led her to begin writing, and she has now published a number of medical romances. She also writes for Enchanted as Trisha David.

Prescription: Romance™

THE BABY AFFAIR
MARION LENNOX

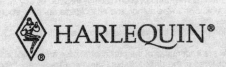

HARLEQUIN®

TORONTO • NEW YORK • LONDON
AMSTERDAM • PARIS • SYDNEY • HAMBURG
STOCKHOLM • ATHENS • TOKYO • MILAN • MADRID
PRAGUE • WARSAW • BUDAPEST • AUCKLAND

ISBN 0-373-63120-0

THE BABY AFFAIR

First North American Publication 1999.

Visit us at www.romance.net

Printed in U.S.A.

CHAPTER ONE

'THERE'S one baby too many in this nursery.'

Sister Ellen Silverton looked up from her desk at sister's station and sighed. Oh, dear. This had to happen. She'd juggled babies and cribs for a week now, but Dr Jock Blaxton wasn't stupid.

In fact, Jock Blaxton was anything but stupid!

Still, maybe she could hang out a little longer. She owed it to Tina to try. Tina Rafter was Gundowring's newest doctor, and if things went wrong then Tina's job could be the briefest in the hospital's history. Ellen thought back briefly to the conversation a week ago. Tina, white-faced and desperate, had been close to breaking point.

'I'll resign, Ellen,' she'd told the charge nurse. 'I can't manage. I can't bring a baby into work.'

'Of course you can,' Ellen had said roundly. 'No one will notice an extra baby.'

No one except Jock Blaxton. Drat the man. He was too intelligent for his own good. The man had eyes in the back of his head. So how could she distract him?

'What on earth do you mean, Jock, dear?' Ellen asked, and then it was Jock's turn to sigh.

'Ellen, don't come the "Jock, dear" with me,' Jock retorted. Gundowring Hospital's obstetrician held up a fistful of patient notes and waved them accusingly at the senior charge nurse. 'There's something going on, and I don't know what. Just because you're twenty years my senior...'

'And I knew your mum.' Ellen sniffed and tried to dredge up a tear, hoping desperately to deflect Jock's attention from one too many cribs. One too many babies...

'Jock, your mother was the nicest lady! She was my very best friend...'

'Ellen!' Jock intensified his glare by a notch or two. 'Stop trying to divert me. Sister Silverton, I want to know what's going on in this nursery, and I want to know *now*!'

'Why, what on earth could be going on?'

What, indeed?

Dr Jock Blaxton frowned at his mother's best friend in frustration. Was he imagining things? Gundowring Hospital was the last place in the world where things 'went on'. It was a busy enough hospital, nestled on the coast of New South Wales and serving a district of over four hundred square miles, but Gundowring was placid and sun-soaked and peaceful.

In fact, Gundowring was too peaceful for Jock Blaxton. Jock had spent the first ten years of his life in Gundowring before his mother died, and he'd returned twenty years later to take the job as hospital obstetrician.

Jock had returned partly because of memories of a happy, sand-and sea-filled childhood and partly because his friend, Struan Maitland, worked here as the hospital's medical director. Struan had been desperate for an obstetrician and hadn't hesitated to twist Jock's arm. And also... Jock had been restless in the city. Searching for something he couldn't even name...

Well, whatever he was searching for he hadn't found it in Gundowring. Jock had tried hard to settle, but twelve months into the job he figured if Gundowring grew any quieter *he'd* grow mould! He'd just returned from a holiday in London, and London was looking good. Dr Jock Blaxton wanted action in life, and he was about to move somewhere he might find it.

For now, though, if Jock wasn't mistaken and he

didn't let Ellen distract him, there was a problem to be dealt with. Action of a sort. One baby too many... What on earth was Ellen playing at?

'OK, if you won't tell me...' Jock lifted the pile of patient histories. 'Let's go through these, shall we, Sister? First.' He read the name from the top history. 'This history belongs to Jody Connor. Jody Connor is two days old.' He looked around until he found the matching crib. 'And Jody's here.' He placed Jody's notes on Jody's pink bassinet and moved on.

Uh-oh... Ellen swallowed and thought fast. Things were getting serious. It was starting to look like Tina was in major trouble.

'I'll...I'll just take little Benjamin in to his mother,' she said, heading for the nearest crib to collect a baby. 'He needs a feed. And Lucy Fleming should go back under the ray lamp...'

Jock placed a hand on Ellen's shoulder and stopped her. 'Leave every single baby where he or she is,' he ordered. 'Ellen—sit!'

'Well, I...'

'Sit!' Jock's powerful hands brooked no opposition. He propelled the senior nurse into her chair.

Defeated, Ellen sat. She glowered. 'You make me sound like a spaniel.'

'You're more like a beagle.' Jock's irresistible grin flashed out, his blue eyes twinkling. 'I know you, Ellen Silverton. You're stubborn, you're wilful and you're very good at playing the innocent. But, Ellen...' He shook his head as Ellen started to rise again. 'No. This nursery's my responsibility. Every night nurse in the place has been sidelining me and I want to know why.'

'If by sidelining you mean avoiding, then I can tell you why,' Ellen muttered darkly. 'Your reputation...'

'My reputation?' Jock was placing a history on each

crib but he was still listening. 'What do you mean—my reputation?'

'If you don't know about your reputation then you have fewer brains than I gave you credit for.' Ellen sighed all over again as she watched Jock move from crib to crib. She'd done all she could. He was going to figure this out. And if he blew the whistle…Would he? Who knew? Certainly not Ellen. After twelve months of working with Jock Blaxton Ellen still didn't think she knew Jock at all.

Once she'd known him well. Jock had been a great little kid, she remembered. Jock's mother had been a real friend of Ellen's, and Jock had grown up with her boys. But at ten his mum had died and his dad had taken it hard. Jock was an only child, dark and intense and deeply troubled by his mother's death. They'd moved to the city. Ellen hadn't seen Jock for twenty years—but then he'd come back to Gundowring, a fully qualified obstetrician, but even more dark and intense than she remembered.

And much, much larger…

He asked about his reputation and Ellen almost groaned. Jock Blaxton was six feet two, with a body to die for. Muscles, muscles and more muscles… Deep black hair. Strongly boned face. Blue-black eyes that were almost shadows. The eyes of an eagle. And a mouth that quirked when you least expected it into laughter so infectious you had to join in.

His patients loved him and every unattached nurse in the hospital was pining for Jock Blaxton—and wondering why he held himself aloof and disappeared to Sydney or overseas every chance he had. He had shadows, Ellen thought sadly. Ghosts from the past that were haunting him. He held himself too far apart. It was as if he was afraid of committing himself to life. To love…

Still, none of this had anything to do with Ellen's

immediate problem. How to explain one extra crib...
She couldn't.

'If I can't take Benjamin to his mother, then I'll just tell his mother what's going on,' she managed, trying to rise again. 'She'll be awake and wondering...'

But Jock wasn't to be deflected. He had one last set of notes in his hand and he'd spotted the matching crib.

'Jason, here are your notes,' he told a week-old baby boy—who wasn't the least bit interested—and then he looked around. There was one crib left over. He was right. There was definitely one baby too many.

'I'll just go—'

'Ellen, stay!' Jock growled—and he walked over to stare down into the one pink crib that didn't have a history on top of the bedclothes.

'I knew I could count,' Jock said in satisfaction, his eyes crinkling in automatic pleasure at the pink-wrapped bundle. 'My maths isn't *that* bad. So, who are you, little one?'

The baby was a tiny girl, maybe four or five weeks old, and she took no notice of Jock at all. Her tiny face was concentrating fiercely on sleep. She had a fuzz of fiery hair, she was finely boned and she was just perfect.

'Ellen..'

'Dr Blaxton, I really must go.' Ellen edged sideways toward the door.

'Nope.' Jock put his big hands into the cot and scooped up the baby. 'Not until you've performed introductions. Who do we have here?'

'I'd have to look at the—'

'History?' Jock finished for her, and his eyes twinkled again. 'Nope again. I've looked at all the histories. There isn't a history for this little one.'

'There must be.'

'Ellen...'

'Look, if you think I have time to waste, trying to...'

Ellen took two steps forward and tried to bluster her way past, but Jock was having none of it. His muscular body blocked her exit.

'Ellen, are we indulging in a spot of moonlighting here?' he asked gently, the twinkle fading. 'Are we doing some child-minding on the side?'

'Don't be silly.'

'Ellen, there's no hospital name-tag on her wrist.' Jock's voice was implacable. 'There's no history and I don't know her. As far as I can remember, I've never seen this little one before.'

'She's Gina's patient,' Ellen gasped, knowing as she uttered the words that she was inviting disbelief. Boy, she was clutching at straws!

Gina was Dr Gina Buchanan—Gundowring's paediatrician. Gina was married to Struan Maitland, the hospital medical director. And Gina and Struan were on holiday.

To fob Jock off by saying this little one was Gina's patient didn't make one ounce of sense. Ellen was, indeed, desperate. Jock shook his head.

'Ellen, you know very well that Gina's away. She and Struan left on long service leave two weeks ago, and before she went Gina handed over to me. She told me of every single patient she has. And she didn't say one thing about a four-week-old girl.'

'She's five weeks old…'

'Five.' Jock nodded, his big hands weighing the baby in his grasp. He had the gentlest hands, Ellen thought. The kindest…

Would he be kind now?

'So you *do* know her,' he said softly. 'Does she have a name?'

Ellen tilted her chin. Daniel facing the lions. It wasn't a bad comparison, she thought. Jock Blaxton was *some* lion.

'Her name's Rose.'

'Rose.' Jock considered. The baby stirred and stretched in her sleep, and her tiny face puckered into a windy smile. Her rosebud lips twitched and Jock smiled despite himself. 'Yeah. I can see why she's called Rose,' he said softly. 'It's a beautiful name for a very beautiful young lady.' And then his voice firmed. 'Ellen, will you tell me just what the hell is going on?'

'I don't—'

'Cut the nonsense, Ellen.' A snap. When Jock meant business he meant business, and Ellen knew the time for dissembling was over. 'I want to know who she is, and I want to know *now*. I want to know what's wrong with her, and if there's nothing wrong with her I want to know why an apparently healthy baby is sleeping in our nursery. Tell.'

'But—'

'Ellen.'

Ellen sighed. And sighed again.

Then, finally, she lifted her face and met Jock's stare. Sister Silverton wasn't intimidated by anyone, lion or not, and she'd known Jock since he was in short pants.

'OK, Jock,' she said softly. 'As I said, her name's Rose, and we're looking after her for Tina.'

Tina.

Jock nearly dropped his bundle. He stared down at the baby in stunned incredulity, and then he stared at Ellen again.

'Tina... You mean Dr Rafter?'

'I mean Dr Rafter,' Ellen said miserably. 'We agreed—'

'Who agreed?'

'Well, I agreed—'

'You agreed to look after Dr Rafter's baby?'

'She'll have to resign as night casualty officer if I

don't,' Ellen told him. 'Jock, you don't understand. Tina's desperate. She can't afford to pay—'

'She can't afford to pay for child-minding?' Jock's voice was still incredulous.

'Jock, you don't understand,' Ellen said again. 'Tina's—'

She got no further. 'Too right, I don't understand.' Jock's face was as black as thunder. 'Of all the nerve. Dr Rafter's only been working here for two weeks. Ellen, we interviewed five applicants for the locum position. There was no mention of a baby.'

Ellen squared her shoulders. 'No. But would it have made a difference?'

'Of course it would. If we'd known she was dependent on us to look after the thing…'

'Dr Blaxton, Rose is *not* a thing!' Ellen's Irish temper was rising fast. 'This baby's called Rose and she's lovely. And you're not to blame Tina. I told her it'd be fine for me to keep Rose here. I also told her not to mention the little one…'

'Why the hell…?'

'Because you know that Wayne Macky will never agree to Tina having the baby here. Not without Struan's say-so, and Struan and Gina are away for three months.'

Jock's eyes widened. 'But Ellen, Tina's just a locum. She has no right to take on a short-term job like this if it involves us looking after her kid.'

But Jock's indignation was met head-on by Ellen's temper. 'That's enough! Tina isn't *just* a locum. You know she's a local girl. We all know her.'

'Well, I don't know her,' Jock said grimly. 'Tina's twenty-eight. She's six years younger than me, which means she would have been all of five years old when I left the district. So, unlike you, I'm not looking at her through rose-coloured glasses.'

'And you don't like her…'

'And I don't like her,' he snapped. 'I've told Struan already that I'm concerned about her having the job. She has no commitment. Even if it is just a locum position I expect dedication, and she's arrived at work late twice already...'

'Jock, Tina has family here. They need her. That's why she wanted the locum position...'

'She said she was between jobs.'

'It's true,' Ellen said desperately, 'but she also needs to spend time with her family. And to look after the little one...'

'And she thought we'd be a soft option.'

'No,' Ellen said flatly. 'Tina knows Wayne Macky, the hospital accountant, would never agree to this. When she took the job she didn't think she'd need child-minding at night, and when she figured it out she wanted to quit. But...' Ellen flushed. 'Well, I knew how much she needed the job and so do all the nurses who work on this ward. We've known Tina for ever. And if you blow the whistle on us...'

'To Wayne, you mean...'

'Yes.' Ellen put her hands on her hips and glared. 'You know Wayne will take it to the hospital board and they'll harrumph about it being irregular and—'

'And kick Dr Rafter and her baby straight out of here.'

'That's right. And if you want to be held responsi-ble—'

'So what's happening here, then?' Jock interrupted grimly. 'Is the staff looking after Rose every night?'

'That's right.'

'The woman's got some nerve.'

'She's got some need!' Ellen snapped. 'I know you don't like Tina, but I don't know why. She's a dear girl. If you were a bit more sympathetic...'

'Ellen, we're not a babysitting service,' Jock said flatly. 'You know we're often tight for beds. And if this little one gets a hospital-based infection like golden staph...'

'Jock...' Ellen bit her lip, unable to defend herself here. It was a definite weak link in her argument. Golden staph was a worry and it had troubled both Ellen and Tina—but, then, Tina really didn't have a choice. Tina knew the risks and it had been sheer desperation which had made her bring Rose in.

'It's not on,' Jock said wearily. 'Hell, Ellen, I won't be responsible for keeping a healthy baby in hospital for the three months of Dr Rafter's term. And it's not fair of her to expect it of us. We pay her a decent wage, and she's old enough to know what she was taking on when she got herself a baby. So now she can just get herself a babysitter.'

'But—'

'No, Ellen.' Jock's arms tightened around the tiny Rose in his arms. 'I know your kind heart. You might not be able to tell her—but I have no such qualms. Cas. is quiet at the moment. I'll take her down and tell her myself.'

'Jock, why don't you like Tina?' Ellen asked Jock quietly, and Jock's mouth tightened into a grim line.

'Because she's a flibbertigibbet and she doesn't take her work seriously,' he retorted. 'And finding out about this little one's existence is exactly what I would have expected of someone like her. I might have guessed about the baby. There had to be a good reason why someone like her would want to leave the city. She'll have to go, and that's all there is to it.'

And he turned on his heel and stalked down the corridor before Ellen could say a word.

Tina Rafter...

Jock walked down the corridor with the grim look intensifying on his face as he walked. Tina...

He'd been against her appointment from the start. She seemed so young... Even though her résumé said she was nearly twenty-nine, it was hard to believe. She seemed too young to be casualty officer, even if it was only short term.

Why had she taken on the job? Jock had known there had to be some reason she was interrupting her career as an anaesthetist to take on a job like this, and it annoyed him that he hadn't been able to figure out what it was.

He couldn't ask her. Jock remembered the day two weeks ago when Struan had brought her into the hospital staffroom for introductions.

Tina had been happy and cheerful and eager to meet everyone, and at first sight Jock had been just as eager to meet her. Tina Rafter was *some* package. She was slight and curvy, with a smile that lit her whole face and with flame-coloured hair that tumbled in gorgeous curls around her shoulders. Her step was light and eager and she'd made an instant, glowing impression.

But then, as Struan had brought her across the room and introduced her to Jock, Tina's face had frozen. The lovely green eyes that faced him were suddenly ice-filled and full of contempt.

Her look had taken Jock aback. He wasn't used to women reacting to him like that. Time after time over the past two weeks he'd told himself that he was imagining it, but he wasn't. The woman had taken an inexplicable dislike to him, and the dislike bordered on contempt.

Jock had voiced his concerns to Struan. Maybe there were problems with the girl that they didn't know about. He'd been overruled. Struan, Wayne Macky and an older member of the hospital board had made the appointment, and they'd known Tina since she was a youngster. They trusted her, even if Jock didn't.

'We might even persuade her to make her position here permanent,' Struan had said as he'd made the last arrangements to take his family off on his long-awaited holiday. 'Her credentials are impeccable and we could use another anaesthetist. She only has the exam to go...'

'That's another thing I don't understand,' Jock had said. 'Why the hell is she interrupting her anaesthetic training to do a locum job?'

'Family problems,' Struan said curtly, and didn't elaborate. 'But see if you can work on her to stay. When Gina and I come back... Well, Gina's doing too much and Lloyd's overworked and there's too much anaesthetics for one person. We could stretch to another doctor.'

Jock could only agree. Especially when he was thinking he wouldn't renew his own contract. But Tina Rafter... The contempt in her eyes disturbed him, as he saw no reason for it. And now... For her not to tell them of her baby... For the woman to be a single mother and not tell them...

Well, maybe he could understand that. Wayne would be unforgiving and old Ron Sergeant, president of the hospital board, would be judgemental. Jock didn't mind the girl having a baby out of wedlock, he decided as he walked grimly down the hospital corridor toward Cas. But if she expected the hospital staff to look after it...

Jock's mouth tightened into a line of decision. He swung open the big glass doors of Cas. and strode in to face her. His timing was unlucky, to say the least. Tina was being solidly, thoroughly, and very, very, passionately kissed. Jock stopped dead and stared—and stared some more.

Who on earth was she kissing? He couldn't see. Tina was slight, five feet five or so, and finely built, with a lovely trim figure. Her skirt and blouse were covered by her customary white medical coat and she was being held against a large male body. All Jock could see of

Tina were her slim, stockinged legs and the mass of fiery red curls, flying free around her shoulders. The rest was enveloped by the man she was kissing.

And the man? He was a farmer at a guess. The kisser was big, rough and grimy, and looked like he'd come straight from the cowyard. As a passionate suitor, Jock thought he left a bit to be desired. Tina didn't think so. She was being kissed and she was kissing right back with heartfelt enthusiasm, and Jock felt his own body stir in recognition of the passion between man and woman.

Anger came to his rescue. Just in time!

'What the hell is going on?'

The kissing couple broke apart reluctantly. There wasn't a lot of guilt here, though. The man turned, Tina held fast within his hold, and Tina was laughing up at him, her green eyes alive with mischief and pleasure.

'Harry Daniel, that's not fair. I said a kiss. I didn't mean an out-of-body experience.'

'I pack a punch,' Harry said placidly, grinning down at the laughing young doctor.

'I'll tell Mary!'

'Yeah, right. You're our chief bridesmaid. She'd never believe you. Besides...' Harry grinned down at Tina in lazy contentment. 'As of next month I intend to spend the next fifty years being faithful to my lovely Mary. This is my last chance to sow wild oats.'

'And that's what I am? Wild oats?'

The big farmer considered and grinned. 'Well, wild... I'd definitely say wild...'

Jock might as well not have been there. He stared. Harry Daniel... He knew him. Local farmer. Local footballer. Engaged to be married to Mary Stevenson, a local schoolteacher.

'What the...?'

Finally he had their attention. They looked across the

room at him and Harry grinned. Tina didn't. As soon as she saw Jock her smile died as if it had never been. She hauled herself out of Harry's clasp and went stiffly back to the sluice tray.

'That's you finished, Harry, lad,' she told him, her voice suddenly tight. 'Come in on Friday and I'll take the stitches out. The scar will fade and we'll have you beautiful for the wedding.'

Jock's eyes swung back to Harry and for the first time he noticed a gauze dressing across the farmer's hand.

'What happened?' he asked, and his incredulity went down a notch.

'I had an argument with a power saw, Doc,' Harry said cheerfully. 'The damned thing won. You never can get the better of those infernal machines.'

'And Dr Rafter was kissing you better?' Jock's voice was tight with disapproval, but Harry didn't bat an eye-lid.

'I told her I'd cry if she didn't.' Harry's grin deep-ened. 'Gave me courage to face the needle and all. She told me she'd give me a kiss better at the end of it if I didn't make a fuss, and I didn't squeal once. Our Dr Rafter's the best. I hope you'll keep her on when her locum's finished, Doc. She cheers the place up no end.' And he gave Tina a cheery wave of his injured hand and took himself off.

Silence.

Behind the desk Barbara, the casualty sister, looked curiously from Jock to Tina and back again. She'd been watching Harry and Tina kiss—and enjoying herself very much indeed—but now she figured that she wasn't wanted in the ensuing conversation. A smart lady was Barbara. She took herself off around the corner to check the reception area—but stayed close enough to the cor-ner to be within earshot.

Tina was clearing the mess from the sluice tray, but

she'd now noticed what Jock was holding, and her hands were on automatic pilot. Her eyes weren't leaving the pink-wrapped bundle of baby in Jock's arms.

The door closed behind Harry, and Tina left her sluice tray and took a step forward.

'Rose,' she said softly, her arms reaching out for the baby. 'Is there something wrong?'

Then she stopped. Jock's face was cold and forbidding, and she had to find the courage to take another step. This wasn't going to work. Ellen had assured her it would. But Tina had known... Sod Jock Blaxton, Tina thought miserably as she looked up into Jock's disapproving face. Sod him! Sod him! Sod him! The man had done so much damage already and here he was, facing her with judgement written all over his face. Well, there was only one way to handle this. Tina was darned if she was going to stand here and face a lecture from Dr Jock Blaxton. No way! She'd told Ellen this wouldn't work, and it hadn't. So get out fast. Cut her losses and go.

'Would you like me to finish my shift before I resign, or would you like me to leave now?' she asked.

More silence.

She'd taken the wind right out of Jock's sails. He stood there without a darned thing to say for himself. He just stared.

'Well?' Somehow Tina made herself take the final steps forward to lift Rose out of his grasp. Rose kept right on sleeping. Tina looked down into the baby's tiny face and felt a surge of love so strong that it threatened to overwhelm her. And this man... He'd done so much damage....

'I'll leave now,' she said.

That made him stir. Jock stared, his anger building. Of all the irresponsible...

'Who's going to look after Casualty?' he demanded. 'Dr Rafter, your contract is for three months.'

'No.'

'What's that supposed to mean?'

'It means I have urgent personal problems, and urgent personal problems sometimes cause contracts to be broken,' Tina snapped. 'In the circumstances, no lawyer will hold me to my contract. And it also means I'm not expecting the least bit of sympathy from you, Jock Blaxton. Ellen told me I was wrong about you, and that you'd react with kindness if you discovered what we were doing. I was a fool to believe her.'

She took a deep breath. 'So... I'll take Rose home now and I'll forfeit my pay up to Thursday. It means you'll be overworked for a couple of days until you find another locum, but I bet that won't kill you, Dr Blaxton. In fact, it might do you good!'

And she turned on her heel and walked to the door.

Somehow Jock stopped her. He took three fast steps forward. As Tina's free hand reached for the brass pull-bar his hand landed on her shoulder and held.

'Just a minute...'

'I'm not listening to lectures from you, Jock Blaxton,' Tina snapped, without turning round. Her hold on the baby in her arms tightened. 'You've messed up this little one's life enough. I was a fool to let her anywhere near you. Now let me go.'

Jock's dark eyes snapped down in a frown. His grasp on Tina's shoulder tightened.

'I don't understand.'

'No. That's your specialty.' And she wrenched herself away.

'Tina...' Jock moved fast, shoving his body between the door and the angry young woman, and his hands swivelled her around to face him. Behind them, the casualty sister, peering round the corner, was practically pop-eyed.

'Look, would you mind telling me what the hell is

going on here?' he demanded. 'I find *my* staff looking after *your* illegitimate daughter—as far as I know, you took this job without even telling us of her existence—and now *you* react with anger, as if we're in the wrong. You've been angry with me from the time we met. And you—'

But Tina was no longer listening.

'My illegitimate daughter?' she gasped. 'My...?'

'What the...?'

But Tina was beyond speaking. She was beyond any reasoned thought at all. She raised her free hand and she slapped him just as hard as she could, a stinging slap right across his face—and then she pushed hard past him, still cradling her little Rose against her breast.

Before Jock could recover, Tina had disappeared out into the car park. Thirty seconds later he heard the sound of a car being gunned into action, and Jock was left, staring after Tina's disappearing tail-lights in absolute bewilderment.

MARION LENNOX 21

gone, oh dear,' he demanded. 'I had my heart leaping
about, your daughter, my daughter—so far as I knew, you
don't look much about even to me... I just can't accept
that you and your twit of a... No, I won't say it, it's too strong.
You need not be so damned... Tell her she's to find Aunt
you.

CHAPTER TWO

THERE was little time for Jock to think about Tina's
crazy reaction for the rest of the night. He was just too
busy. There was normally only one doctor on duty in
the hospital overnight and the night casualty officer was
it. Night casualty officer. Dr Tina Rafter, no longer employed. Specialists were called in at need. Tina's sudden
departure meant that Jock had to act as casualty officer
for the rest of the night, as well as perform his normal
obstetric work if needed.

He was needed. So Jock fixed drips, coped with a
heart attack, dealt with an old lady who was frantic because she couldn't sleep and didn't wish anyone else to
sleep if she couldn't—and delivered a baby. The delivery was tricky, needing high forceps, and by seven in
the morning Jock was close to exhaustion.

He finished stitching the new mother's perineum, and
then ended up back in the nursery to recheck his new
arrival just as Ellen was doing change-over, ready to
leave.

Sister Silverton took one look at Jock and her normally benign face creased into disapproval and anger. In
a small country hospital the nurse-doctor lines of au-
thority were smudged, and the fact that Ellen had
bounced Jock on her knee when he was tiny meant the
lines here were non-existent.

Now Sister Silverton was angry, and the world was
about to hear of it.

'Dr Blaxton, you had no need to dismiss Dr Rafter,'
she snapped. 'Sister in Casualty told me what happened.
Dismissing Tina out of hand, without even asking for an

explanation... Jock, if your mother could see you now she'd be ashamed of you.'

Jock closed his eyes. He'd been up Sunday night with a delivery, he'd spent most of Monday consulting, Monday night had just finished and he was facing Tuesday exhausted beyond belief. He'd had enough!

'Ellen, I did not dismiss Tina,' he said through gritted teeth. 'She left. She walked out. Broke her contract and departed. And it's good riddance, as far as I can see.'

Ellen's breath sucked in fast.

'You don't mean that.'

'I do. She's flighty, she flirts with patients, she's not punctual, she's incompetent and, as well as that, she expects this hospital to look after her illegitimate child because she's too irresponsible to look after her herself. Or too mean to pay for childcare. Where the father is, I have no idea. I wouldn't be surprised if she doesn't even *know* who the father is!'

Ellen stared.

'Now, if you're quite finished, could you arrange for Mr Macky to contact the locum agency to find a replacement for Dr Rafter before you go off duty,' Jock said wearily. 'I need to have some breakfast and I have an elective Caesar booked in at eight.'

Ellen stared some more, and finally found her tongue.

'Did she hit you?' she asked softly. There were still four red finger-marks across Jock's cheek, but Ellen's voice wasn't the least bit sympathetic. 'Barbara said she hit you. Did Tina hit you hard?'

'Yes, she did,' Jock snapped. 'I could have her up for assault. Of all the—'

He got no further. Ellen Silverton walked straight over and gave Jock a ringing, stinging slap on the other cheek.

'That's from your mother,' Ellen told him harshly. 'And from me. And if you'd like to dismiss me, too, then go right ahead. I'm too old to pander to the likes of you, Dr Blaxton. Of all the arrogant, overbearing, judgemental... You should be ashamed of yourself.'

'*I* should...'

'Yes, *you* should.' Ellen put her hands up to grip Jock's shoulders and pushed him down hard onto her chair. He was so astounded that his long legs buckled under him—and he sat. 'You shut up, Jock,' Ellen snapped. 'Sit down and shut up and listen.'

'But—'

'Not one word until I'm through.' Ellen was small and broad and red-faced with fury. She stood before him like an avenging angel.

'One,' she snapped. 'Tina is a dear girl and what she's gone through... What she's facing...'

'I don't—'

'Shut up, Dr Blaxton,' Ellen said thunderously. 'Second. Rose Maiden is not Tina's daughter. The baby is Tina's niece. Tina's sister's child. If you accused Tina of being an irresponsible mother of an illegitimate child, when she's carrying the weight of the world on her shoulders, then it's no wonder she slapped you. And to accuse her of promiscuity...'

'She was kissing Harry Daniel in Casualty...'

Ellen took a deep breath, fighting for control.

'Yes, so Barbara tells me. She says you reacted like an outraged lover. Dr Blaxton, Tina and Harry have been close friends since pre-school, and next month Harry is marrying Mary, Tina's best friend from high school. So she kissed him. That makes her promiscuous?'

'But...' It was Jock's turn to fight for breath here. Things were spinning way out of control, and it was starting to look possible that he just might have made a fool of himself. 'But... If Rose isn't Tina's daughter...'

'I told you. Rose is Tina's sister's baby.'

'Then why isn't Tina's sister looking after her own baby?'

'She can't. Christie was admitted to hospital in Sydney a week ago, suffering from exhaustion and severe postnatal depression.'

'I don't—'

'You don't what?' Ellen snapped. 'You don't believe it? You'd rather believe that our Tina is a promiscuous, unreliable tramp? Is that it?' Ellen shook her head. 'And I thought you were a decent man, Jock. I'm ashamed of you, and your mother would turn in her grave if she could see how you'd turned out.'

And Ellen turned on her heel and started to walk away.

'Ellen…'

Jock's voice stopped her dead. There was weary desperation in Jock's voice. And also…also horror.

'Ellen, I think you need to tell me what's going on,' Jock said slowly. He fingered his bruised cheek and winced. 'OK,' he admitted, as she turned back to face him. 'I may have jumped to a few conclusions. But… Ellen, if I'm to avoid bruises all over me, maybe I need to know what's really going on.'

Ellen pursed her lips, still angry. 'Dr Blaxton, it's not my business…'

'Ellen.'

'Yes?'

'Sit. And tell. Please. Who is Tina's sister?'

Ellen sighed. OK. Jock's 'please' had had real desperation behind it. Maybe everything wasn't lost here. Maybe if she made an effort…

'Tina's sister is a woman called Christine Maiden,' she told him. 'She lives just out of town.'

'I see.' Jock didn't yet, but he was trying hard. 'So…Christine had her baby—Rose—here five weeks ago?'

'Yes.'

'That must have been while I was on holiday in London.'

It still didn't make sense, though. Jock frowned. As the only obstetrician in the district, he knew all the pregnant ladies around here. Or he'd thought he did. And he hadn't heard of a Christine Maiden.

'So…did Henry Roddick deliver her?' Henry was the relief obstetrician to whom Jock paid a fortune to look after his practice while he was away.

'If you didn't deliver her, then I guess Henry must have,' Ellen told him. 'I'd assumed you had. Tina told me it was you. But I was on leave then too.'

'But…' Jock shook his head, as if trying to clear a fog. 'If she had the baby here—if Christine's a local— then why don't I know her? I was only away for two weeks. If she lives near here, who did her prenatal checks?'

'Well…she might not have had any,' Ellen said diffidently. 'She was in trouble from the start.'

'Why?'

Ellen shrugged and sighed. And then spread her hands. 'It's a bit of a long story.'

'So try me.'

'Well, I don't know it all,' Ellen said slowly, 'but I gather… Tina says Christie's husband walked out when she was two months pregnant. They live on a farm about ten miles out of town and barely make ends meet. There's already a four-year-old and a two-year-old. Instead of trying to find help, Christie struggled on through the pregnancy by herself. Hardly anyone in town knew she was pregnant. I didn't. We never saw her.'

'But she ended up in Henry's care for the delivery?'

'I guess.'

'Do we have notes?'

'They'll be with your patient files,' Ellen said diffidently. 'You can look them up—if you want.'

'You don't think I will?' Jock's frown darkened. 'You don't think I give a toss?'

'I didn't say that.'

'I figured your opinion out all by myself.' Jock fingered his aching cheek with a rueful smile. 'I'm clever like that. Hit me hard enough and I'll figure you disapprove. Hell, Ellen, you could have told me all this before... So where does this leave Tina?'

'She's taking care of all of them,' Ellen told him. 'All the children. She took the locum job here because she was worried about her sister, and then when she arrived Christie just fell in a heap. So Tina had her admitted to hospital for rest and recuperation. Which leaves Tina with sole care of the children. I gather Tina's paying a girl to live in so she can get some sleep during the day, but the girl won't get up to a five-week-old baby at night. So Tina's bringing Rose with her to work.'

'And who knows about it?'

'Only the nurses on this ward.'

'Not Gina and Struan?'

'No. At least... Struan knew why Tina came home, but he didn't know she was bringing Rose to work.'

'Why not?'

Ellen shrugged. 'Christie wasn't in hospital when they left. And, anyway, Tina thinks the less people who know her sister's in a psychiatric hospital the better. This is a small town and it's judgemental.' She shrugged again. 'Well, maybe not so judgemental but Christie's afraid of stigma. Apparently, she wouldn't even go to a doctor here to seek help. Tina had to take her to Sydney.'

'Hell!'

'It is, isn't it?' Ellen said mildly. Flatly. Not letting him off the hook one bit. 'And you've just made it much, much worse. Now, if you'll excuse me, Doctor, I'd best be off. If you want me to contact the locum agency before I go home to bed...'

'Leave it,' Jock said heavily. He raked his fingers through his thick black curls in a gesture of absolute weariness. 'Can you...? Ellen, can you ask Tina if she'll come back? Say I understand about the baby?'

'No.' Ellen shook her grey head decisively.

'Why not?'

'Because if you want her to come back, I have a suspicion that it's you who'll have to ask her to return,' Ellen told him. 'She's a proud girl is Tina. You sacked her, Dr Blaxton. You fix it.'

It was five o'clock that afternoon before Jock found time to get to Tina's sister's farm. He'd found the address from the patient notes, but the address was vague and it took him half an hour to reach the farm. Even then he wasn't sure he was at the right place. Jock climbed from his car to open the farm gate and he looked up at the house in dismay. Surely no one could live here?

The house was a ramshackle cottage set high on the ridge where the coastal plains turned to rugged mountains. Here the bush was fast encroaching on the cleared land. The cottage was fenced off from the bush but there were eucalypts suckering everywhere, and masses of bracken clustering closer and closer to the house.

There were scrawny chickens on the front verandah and one sad-looking cow, staring moodily down the track at Jock's neat little sports car. Was he in the right place? Jock nearly turned away, but then there was a shout of laughter from the back of the cottage. A girl's chuckling voice calling out.

'I spy Ally...'

And Tina burst from behind the cottage. This wasn't the neat, white-coated and professional doctor Jock had seen in the hospital, though. Tina was dressed now in scruffy jeans and T-shirt, with a bundle cradled against her breast. She was barefooted and her flame-red hair was flying. With one hand steadying her bundle, she raced up the verandah steps to the front door, where she thumped the panels with a resounding bang.

'Home. *Out!* That's it, Ally Maiden. Tim and I have found you and now you're *It*!' And then she swooped back down the steps to the side of the house to where a child was toddling after her. Still steadying her bundle, she scooped the little boy up onto her hip with her free arm and hugged him hard. 'How about that, Tim, boy?' She gave a war whoop of triumph and spun toddler, bundle and herself in a circle. 'We've found Ally.'

But Tim had seen Jock. The little boy stared out at Jock's sleek little Alfa sports car and his jaw dropped.

'Car, Aunty Tina. *Car!*'

Aunty Tina turned to look—and froze. Unlike Tim, she didn't see the sleek little sports car. She only saw Jock. Dr Jock Blaxton. In person. Jock Blaxton here! This was her worst nightmare come to haunt her. Then Ally came racing round the house—a little girl of about four with hair the same flaming red as her aunt's.

'I thought you'd never find me,' the child was crowing happily. 'I hid for ages and ages...'

Then she, too, saw Jock. She stopped and stared—and then she headed straight for Tina and grabbed her hand, which left Tina standing stupidly on the verandah steps, one baby slung in a papoose against her breast, one child on her hip and one child clutching her hand—all of them waiting for Jock to approach.

When all Tina wanted to do was walk inside and slam the door. If she did slam the door, the whole place would fall down, she thought ruefully. There wasn't anywhere secure you could hide around here. If ever a big bad wolf could blow a house down, this was the house.

Jock was walking up the track, the warm wind ruffling

his thatch of deep black hair and his blue-black eyes creased against the afternoon sun. The big bad wolf in person. Tina backed up the steps, the children clutched close. *She looks afraid*, Jock thought suddenly. *Why on earth…?*

'Tina?' He stopped at the foot of the steps and looked up at the little group, standing by the front door. Tina didn't blame him one bit for not coming further. The steps looked like they might collapse at any minute.

'That's me,' she said, her voice carefully neutral. Then she turned to her niece, forcing herself to make an effort. To try and find *something* to say. 'Ally, this is Dr Blaxton. He's the man I told you about who was so horrid to me this morning. Dr Blaxton, this is my niece, Alison—better known as Ally—and this is my nephew, Timothy.'

Jock found himself being regarded by four large, very interested and totally judgemental eyes. Ally's small chin tilted straight up, defiance in every inch of her person. Dr Blaxton. She knew all about Dr Blaxton.

'You made my Aunty Tina cry,' she said severely. 'We don't like you, Dr Blaxton. Even if your car *is* nice, I think you'd better go away from here.'

Jock swallowed. This wasn't getting any easier.

'I didn't mean to make your Aunty Tina cry.'

'Then why did you?'

'I made a mistake.'

Six eyes were watching him. Maybe eight if you counted the baby, swathed snugly against Tina's breast. All were the same intense green, with the same light behind. All were redheads. You could have sworn these children belonged to this girl.

'Did you come to say you're sorry?' Ally asked curiously, and Tina made a sharp little movement backwards.

'He doesn't need to say he's sorry, Ally,' she said grimly. 'I don't want him to apologise.'

'He made you cry.'

'I was silly,' Tina said flatly. 'Silly to let him upset me. Dr Blaxton doesn't have anything to do with us. He shouldn't be able to make any of us cry.' Then she tilted her own chin and the eyes that met Jock's were cold and hard.

'Please leave,' she said flatly.

'Tina, I'm sorry...' Jock's voice was getting a bit desperate. He didn't know what he was fighting here, and he wasn't enjoying the sensation one bit. 'I shouldn't have implied that Rose was your daughter... It was—'

'Is that all you've come to apologise for?' Tina asked incredulously. 'Is that all? Implying that I might have an illegitimate daughter? You hurt us in every way possible and that's all...' Her voice broke off, strangled in impotent fury, and there was a long, drawn-out silence. Not even the children spoke. Finally Jock found his voice.

'Tina, I don't have a clue what you're talking about.'

Tina stared, and stared some more, as if she couldn't believe her eyes. 'You mean you don't know what damage you've done?'

'No.' There was nothing else to say to her question, but that one word was enough to open the floodgates.

'You don't know...' Tina's green eyes flashed fire. 'You don't know! You admit my sister into hospital, deliver her baby and discharge her twenty-four hours later—*twenty-four hours!*—because she's a public patient and you can only charge the set amount for delivery no matter how long she stays in hospital. And she's exhausted almost to death, she's starving herself, she's depressed beyond measure and she has no one at home to help—*no one*! But you send her away because you can't make any more money out of her, and you don't give a damn.'

Tina might only be five feet five inches high, but what she lacked in stature now she more than made up for in venom. She was practically spitting.

'And you don't even follow through. Not even with the easy things. You don't contact the maternal child care centre and send a home visitor. There's no one to care. My sister came home here after one night in hospital and the neighbour handed back these two and left her. No one even contacted me until two weeks later, and then I flew down from Brisbane to find...'

Tina gasped and choked and then closed her eyes, remembering a nightmare. 'Well, it was just as well that I came.' She pulled the two little ones closer. 'Mummy was ill, wasn't she, kids? But now she's in hospital and she'll be better soon. But we don't need your apology, Dr Blaxton. My sister needed a caring doctor and she didn't get one. So now... We don't need you now. We don't need you at all. So I think you'd best leave before I get even angrier.'

Silence. More silence. It stretched on for ever. A mopoke called from high in the gum trees around the house. The call was high and mournful, accusing. The whole world, it seemed, was accusing Jock Blaxton.

Maybe the bird was right to be accusing. Maybe Tina was right. Hell! Jock's feeling of weariness intensified almost past bearable limits. He was responsible here, horribly responsible. Maybe he wasn't as responsible as Tina believed, but he was responsible enough. He'd badly wanted a holiday and he'd hired Henry Roddick without any guarantees as to the man's competency. He'd expected Gina and Struan to keep an eye on him— but maybe they'd been just too busy.

'Tina, I didn't deliver your sister's baby,' Jock said softly, his voice laced with exhaustion. 'I've been away, overseas. Did your sister tell you definitely that it was me who delivered her?'

Tina's eyes widened.

'That's crazy. Yes, she did. Dr Blaxton...'

'Are you sure she didn't find out who the obstetrician here was some time during her pregnancy, and then just assumed Dr Roddick was me? If she was so distressed...' Jock's voice softened still further. 'If she was so distressed when she was having the baby, maybe she didn't listen to introductions during labour.'

'I don't...' Tina looked blank. 'I guess...'

Jock's voice firmed in the face of her uncertainty. 'Tina, it definitely was Dr Roddick who delivered her. After Ellen told me Rose was your sister's child, I looked up your sister's history. Christie hasn't been near me. I haven't seen her once through her whole pregnancy. According to Henry's notes, there was no prenatal history at all. Her delivery caught Henry by surprise. She delivered normally, and requested discharge twenty-four hours later. He saw no reason why she shouldn't be discharged.'

Tina's mouth dropped open. Her huge eyes practically enveloped her face.

'You mean... It wasn't you.'

'It wasn't me.'

Tina's eyes closed in denial.

'Oh, no... Oh, no!'

'I think...maybe we've both done ourselves an injustice here,' Jock said wearily. 'Maybe we should start again and figure out just what happened.'

Tina's eyes opened cautiously. 'But... I made you stay up all night,' Tina said slowly. 'You had a woman in labour, and you had all my casualty patients as well. You must have been so busy...'

'I survived.'

'I hit you.'

'I deserved it.'

'No, you didn't,' Tina said honestly. 'I had no right to take Rose to work. Ellen talked me into it. But—'

'But I should have found out the whole story, before flying off the handle.'

'Excuse me!' It was a virtuous voice from waist height. Four-year-old Ally had been looking from her aunt to Jock with increasing impatience. 'Excuse me, Aunty Tina, but are you making friends with Dr Blaxton?'

'I don't know.' Tina managed the ghost of a smile. 'I'm thinking about it.'

'I thought we hoped Dr Blaxton got something... something with pox in it.'

'Never mind, Ally,' Tina cut in hastily. 'We don't hope any such thing any more. I might have made a mistake about Dr Blaxton.'

'Does that mean we can have a ride in his car?'

Tina gasped and choked. Suddenly the smile was flooding back—the smile that Jock had seen directed at other people but never at himself. The smile that had had him entranced from the moment he'd seen it and had made Tina's contempt all the more hurtful. And now her smile was flooding straight at him.

'Oh, Ally... Oh...' Tina shook her head, and there was the glimmer of tears behind her smile. 'Oh, heck...' She put her nephew down on his two sturdy little legs, the baby swaying against her breast as she bent, and then she straightened and held out her hand towards Jock. 'Dr Blaxton, you can't know how good it feels not to need to hate you,' she told him.

Ditto.

That smile was doing strange things to Jock's solar plexus. He took Tina's firm, cool hand in his, and the things kept on happening, only faster. This was a girl unlike any he'd ever met before. Tina wasn't wearing a scrap of make-up. Her eyes were clear and bright and honest, and she was up to her neck in domesticity. There were milk stains on both her shoulders and the baby slung against her breast looked like she belonged there. This was the sort of scene that would normally make Jock run a mile!

'How's...how's Rose?' he managed, and his voice sounded only slightly hoarse. Only slightly out of kilter...

'As you see.' Tina smiled fondly down at her bump. 'She'll let us do anything as long as we take her along. Very sociable, our Rose. But at the moment she's fast asleep. Long may it last.'

'Why...?' Hell, how to get his voice working properly? 'Why isn't she in hospital with her mother?' In cases of severe postnatal depression it usually made things worse to separate mother and child. 'I don't understand,' Jock complained. There was so much here he didn't understand, not least of which was the way the girl in front of him made his legs feel—sort of like jelly. It was those eyes... But Tina's face was closing again, pain washing back.

'I don't think...' She sighed and the light faded from those brilliant eyes. 'Maybe you don't understand just how ill my sister was when I found her,' she said softly. She flicked Ally's crimson curls. 'Ally, can you take Tim and collect some eggs? If we make Dr Blaxton an omelette and treat him really well, then maybe he'll give you and Tim a ride in his car.'

'Really?' Four avid eyes looked straight up at Jock, their faces a picture.

Who could resist? Jock spread his broad hands and let his eyes crinkle into a smile of agreement. This little group was like a fine silk net, drawing him in. He should go straight home to bed, but these matching sets of green eyes...

Irresistible.

'Really.' Jock grinned, caving right in. 'For a farm-egg omelette, a car ride is a small price to pay.'

'Oh, boy!' Ally gave a war whoop to match Tina's. She grabbed her brother's hand and both children swooped off toward the hen-house.

Jock was left with Tina...and one baby...

CHAPTER THREE

THEY stood in the late afternoon sun, neither knowing where to start. Tina's bare toes shifted uncomfortably on the dusty verandah boards while Rose stirred and then settled against her breast. Tina winced. She loved the feeling of Rose, but Jock made her feel... He made her feel young. Gauche. Out of her depth.

'Come in and have some lemonade,' she said at last, and her words were strained. 'That is...well, I seem to have hijacked you for dinner. Can you bear it?'

'To have a home-cooked omelette and take two kids for a ride in my car?' Jock's lazy smile swung back into action. 'I can bear it.' He followed her inside the cottage, and part of him was acknowledging that at least some of his willingness sprang from Tina's neatly packaged body. She looked great in jeans and bare toes. Immersed in domesticity, with or without baby, she looked just great!

Inside, the cottage was much like outside. Grinding poverty stared at him from every angle. Jock stopped at the kitchen door and stared around him. There'd been attempts to keep it neat. The house was clean—but that was about all that could be said for it. The furniture was almost non-existent. There was a table, of sorts, but no chairs. The seating consisted of a pile of wooden fruit crates. The floor covering had given up the ghost long ago. A strip of linoleum lay before an ancient wood stove, but the rest of the floor was bare, scrubbed boards.

A bunch of bottlebrush in a jam jar gave the room its only colour—a bright splash of crimson that went perfectly with Tina's wondrous hair. It made the place seem as if someone cared. Someone did. Tina was watching Jock's face and she saw his eyes rest on the bottlebrush.

'We change the flowers every morning,' she said, her hand soothing Rose with semi-conscious strokes. 'It makes us all feel better.'

'Why…?' Jock shook his head and lowered his frame gingerly onto a fruit crate. 'Tina, why is your sister living like this? This is dreadful. She surely doesn't need to. There are social agencies who can help. They'll give her furniture at least.'

'They will.' Tina's mouth set into a tight line. 'They will now. But they haven't been allowed to.'

'Can I ask why not?'

Tina shrugged. She filled the kettle and placed it on the stove, then pulled up her own fruit box to the table, settling herself and the baby to face Jock Blaxton. To share a truth that hurt.

'My sister's proud,' she told him. 'She's always been stubborn and strong and totally in control. Only now…'

'Now?'

'Christie's husband has been having an affair with another woman,' Tina said bluntly, meeting Jock's eyes head-on. 'With a teenager, for heaven's sake. Christie found out when she was two months pregnant. Ray…Christie's husband…wanted her to get an abortion, even though the baby was planned.'

'And she refused?'

'Of course Christie refused.' Tina looked down at Rose as though the thought was totally abhorrent. Which it was. She smiled softly at the downy little head and bent her head to give the faint tinge of red hair a soft kiss. 'Christie wanted this baby. She loves her kids. She loves… She loved Ray.'

'So?'

Tina sighed. 'So Christie took the children away for a few days to give her time to think. In retrospect, it was a stupid move. I think she'd expected Ray to panic—to come after her. But he didn't. And when she finally came back Ray had stripped the place bare. He'd sold everything that was of any value at all. Everything. Even the floor coverings. He'd cleared out their bank accounts. He'd run up debt on their credit cards and he'd gone. He even took every single light bulb in the place.'

'Oh, no...'

'And, instead of calling for help, Christie just froze,' Tina went on sadly. 'Our parents died some years ago. I was up in Brisbane, working, and she didn't tell me anything was wrong.'

'But you must have known...'

'How could I know?' Tina's eyes clouded with pain. 'I was so busy with my own life—with my medicine— and I thought... Well, Christie didn't even tell me she was pregnant. I hadn't seen her since last Christmas. I'd ring her and she'd chat normally about Ray and the kids—as if there was nothing wrong.'

'So what did she do for money?'

'I don't know,' Tina said grimly. 'As far as I can see, she didn't even apply for social welfare. She had the poultry and the cow so at least the kids had eggs and milk. But she didn't go near the neighbours, and the few friends she had she wouldn't see. Because she was so embarrassed...'

Jock closed his eyes, thinking it through. A woman struggling with the emotional turmoil of pregnancy as well as a whole life shattered. If ever a woman had needed a caring doctor, Christie had. But Christie had used no doctor at all.

'And then she had Rose...'

'She had to ask for help then.' Tina's voice was bleak, and Jock knew she was kicking herself for not being here. For not having guessed something was wrong. 'She didn't have a car—it had been leased and there was no money to meet the payments—so when she went into labour she walked over to the nearest neighbour and asked her to take her to the hospital. The neighbour isn't particularly kind, but when she saw the state Christie was in…well, the woman knows me a little. When Rose was two weeks old she managed to track me down and said…just that I ought to come.'

'And you did.' Jock's eyes were open again now. He was watching Tina, watching her haunted face. Watching the pain behind her eyes. Watching the expressions flit from bleakness to despair.

'I did—and Christie was almost dead,' Tina told him, and Jock knew she was hardly registering that he was there at all. She was only seeing Christie. 'Christie was feeding them all but she was doing nothing else. She was barely talking and she wasn't feeding herself. I tried to take her to hospital here but she just disintegrated. So I took her down to Sydney.'

'Without the baby?'

'There's no problem about Christie bonding with Rose,' Tina said bleakly, 'But…what she desperately needs is time for herself. Time to recover her strength and start thinking about the future. Time to figure out that there is life after what's happened to her.'

'Time to figure that there's life after pride,' Jock said softly, and Tina's eyes flew to his face.

'You understand,' she said wonderingly. Her eyes met his across the table, and Tina found herself fighting an unexpected feeling of warmth. She'd been alone with this nightmare for so long and now… Now comfort was coming from a source where she'd least expected it.

More than comfort. A feeling of… A feeling she didn't understand in the least, as though this man was part of her.

Good grief! She shook her head as if she didn't understand herself. She didn't. 'It's just…it seems crazy,' she faltered, trying hard to get a grip on herself. 'But Christie's always been so strong. She's always been a mover and shaker. For this to happen... It shook her foundations, brought her crashing down. She's so ill...'

'How long will she be in hospital?'

'I might bring her home next week,' Tina said doubtfully. 'The kids and I are going to see her on Sunday.' She hesitated. 'Though I guess I could take them to see her now... Now I don't have a job.'

'You do have a job.' Jock reached over the table and gripped her hands. The feeling of her soft hands in his was...well...great! 'Hell, Tina... You're as bad as Christie. To not tell anyone...'

'I did tell people,' Tina told him. She looked down at their linked hands for a long moment, as if trying to figure out where the warmth was coming from. From where the comfort was flowing. Finally it seemed to register that her hands had been there too long, and she hauled them away reluctantly. And Jock was just as reluctant to release them.

'I told Ellen and Struan and Gina,' she continued, only a slight flush of crimson showing that she had been aware of the warmth between their hands. 'Struan knew why I wanted the locum job and then, when Christie had to go into hospital, I told Ellen what was happening. She told the rest of the night shift nurses. Christie will hate it, but people have to know.'

'You could have told me.'

'Not when—'

'Not when you thought it was me who'd treated Christie like this,' Jock said grimly, meeting her look directly across the table. 'Discharging her without checking...'

'I'm sorry.' Tina took a deep breath, forcing herself to concentrate on the man before her rather than on her sister's troubles. And forcing herself to concentrate on what he was saying rather than on the strange sensations she was starting to feel.

'Jock, I'm so sorry I thought it was you,' she told him in a voice that wasn't quite steady, 'but Christie was definite that it was you who delivered her. And... Well, whoever it was, he needs to be struck off.' Tina's voice was tight with pain. She looked across at Jock, willing him to understand.

'Jock, Christie was anorexic. She weighs seven stone, for heaven's sake. They weighed her when she was admitted in Sydney. For him not to see... And you hired him,' she added, a flash of the old fire shooting out Jockwards.

'I know. I accept responsibility there.' Jock gave a rueful grimace. 'Hell, Tina, I didn't get it right. But tell me how I can get it right now.' He looked searchingly over the table at her. She seemed such a slip of a girl to have this burden thrust on her—to be inundated with kids and responsibility. He kept on looking and his gut gave a savage twist. For him to have caused such pain... What price a holiday to London? 'How can I help now?' he asked.

Tina's response was fast and to the point.

'Give me my job back.'

'Of course.' Jock frowned. 'But... Tina, should you be working at all? You have your hands full.'

'I do,' Tina admitted, 'but I'm almost as broke as Christie.'

'I don't understand.' Jock's frown deepened. 'You've been qualified for a while now. You won't have been earning peanuts.'

'Would you believe I have massive gambling debts?' Tina's irrepressible twinkle flashed out and Jock blinked. For her to laugh... For her to have all this on her shoulders and to *laugh*!

'No.' He barely managed a matching smile. His gut

was doing strange wrenching things that he didn't understand at all. 'I wouldn't believe it. So tell me the truth.'

Tina hesitated but only for a second. Her finances had nothing to do with Jock. Her family had nothing to do with Jock, but the warmth behind his dark eyes told her that he really wanted to know, and his concern was irresistible. In fact, Jock Blaxton was irresistible.

Outside, they could hear the children laughing together as they carried the eggs toward the house.

'We've got seven,' Ally was shouting. 'Seven!'

'Car!' said Tim. 'Car.'

'We'll put the eggs down here and have a look at the car,' Ally said seriously. 'But just for a minute, Tim, 'cos Aunty Tina's waiting.'

So was Jock. Waiting for Tina to tell him everything.

'Our parents died I was sixteen and Christie was nineteen,' Tina told him slowly, her eyes still on his face. 'I worked my way through medical school, but I couldn't cover all my expenses. Christie helped—which is one of the reasons I feel so bad now. So responsible that she's broke. But I also had to borrow and I'm still paying off loans. Much as I'd like to spend the next six months with Christie and the children, I can't afford to.'

'Let me help.'

Tina looked oddly across the table at him.

'With another loan?' She shook her head. She found that easy enough to resist. 'No. Thank you, Dr Blaxton, but no.'

'What would you like to do now?' Jock demanded. 'If money was no object.'

'That's crazy. I can't—'

'Just tell me.'

This man... He had such a magnetic, powerful personality. It was as if somehow he could wave a magic wand and make everything better. Which, of course, he

couldn't. No one could, not even the great Jock Blaxton.
But Jock was waiting for an answer to his ridiculous
question.

'I guess… If I had my druthers, I'd take the children
to Sydney until Christie is well enough to come home.
And then I'd continue working here the way I have
been.'

'Taking Rose into work with you? Paying someone to
be here?'

'That's right.'

'It won't work.'

'I know. I can't afford—'

'Regardless of what you can and can't afford, you
can't take Rose back into the hospital,' Jock said firmly.
'Christie doesn't want a baby with golden staph, and I
don't want a nursery of children infected by a child
who's in and out of the community. No. This is what
you'll do.'

'I beg your pardon—'

'Tina, the locum I hired helped cause this mess.' Jock
was watching the girl on the other side of the table in-
tently, as if trying to figure out the workings of a strange
and unfamiliar piece of machinery. Some machinery! 'If
you were a different sort of person then you could sue
the pants off me.'

Good grief! Tina's eyes flew to Jock's face and she
gave an involuntary choke of laughter. Suing the pants
off Jock Blaxton… It had its appealing points. *Good
grief!* Her colour rose.

'I wouldn't—'

'No. But you could sue Henry for negligence and un-
professional conduct, and that would embarrass me professionally. As you say, I hired him and I'm responsible
for his actions. So we'll settle out of court.'

'I told you, Dr Blaxton, I won't—'

'Tina, I'm settling with your sister. Not you.'

'But—'

'Shut up, Tina,' Jock said kindly. 'You might not have much money, but I do. I've been qualified for years and I'm single. I spend my money on cars and not much else. So... There's a lady living a couple of miles down the road from here and she's looking for a job. She has an outdated mothercraft nursing qualification. She's only just moved here and she came into the hospital last week to see if there was any work. Until she upgrades her qualifications there isn't work for her at the hospital, but there is here. So...'

'Jock, I—'

'Shut up,' he said again. 'I'm not doing this for you, Tina Rafter. I'm doing it for your sister, and you have no right to refuse on her behalf. So I'll employ Marie to work here. Full time, sleeping over as needed. She'll do it and she'll love it. And the kids will love her.'

'But—'

'You take the kids down to Sydney, bring Christie home and settle everything down. Make sure you're happy with Marie. Then come back to work.'

'I can't take time off.'

'You resigned,' Jock said firmly. 'You resigned in front of witnesses. So now you can't come back until I say so. And that's not until everyone's ready. Until Christie and Marie are coping with the children.'

'You can't take my workload...'

'I'll share your workload with the others.' Jock gave an inward shrug. So much for spending time searching for a replacement for his own job, as he'd intended. Somehow it didn't matter so much now. Not when Tina's eyes were watching him with a trace of hope behind her despair. 'We've coped with a shortage of medical staff before and we'll do it again. Don't argue, Dr Rafter. Just do it.'

'Jock, I can't.'

But Jock simply reached across the table and took her hands in his again. That one simple action took her breath away. It stopped her protests dead.

'Yes, you can,' he said gently. 'You can, Tina. Your responsibility is to your sister and to her children. And, because of my dreadful locum, I share that responsibility. So move over and let me share.'

'Jock...' Tina looked helplessly up into Jock's eyes and was lost, hopelessly, bewilderingly lost. Half an hour ago she'd hated this man. And now... Now he was gripping her fingers and her body was doing all sorts of strange things in return—and she didn't know whether she was Arthur or Martha. Martha, she thought suddenly, very definitely Martha. If Jock was Arthur.

He was expecting her to speak when it was as much as she could do to get her mouth open. Worse, she had to think of something intelligent to say. Ally and Tim saved her. They'd obviously finished their car inspection. They burst through the door, bearing a bowl full of eggs, and they stopped short when they saw their Aunty Tina holding hands across the table with this interesting man, the owner of the wonder car.

'You're holding hands,' Ally said, and she frowned, working things out. 'Does this mean you're going to be friends?'

Tina tried to drag her hands away, but Jock would have none of it.

'Yes, Ally, it means just that,' Jock said solemnly, and it was as if he were taking a vow. His grip on Tina's slender fingers tightened. 'It means that from now on your Aunt Tina and I are definitely friends. For just as long as it takes to get you guys all back together again as a family.'

Or maybe longer?

Family.

After eating a wonderful omelette and taking the two

children for a drive along the track leading to the house—he'd sat them on his knee one at a time and let them steer, and the kids were now friends for life—Jock drove home from Tina's dilapidated cottage, and for some reason the word kept resounding in his head.

Family.

It sounded good. No, it didn't, Jock told himself savagely, hauling his head back into line. It sounded claustrophobic. It sounded like prison. Family meant committing yourself to one person, and committing yourself to one person meant kids, mortgage, school fees—the full catastrophe. And then something would happen, as it had for Christie and as it had for Jock's parents. One partner walks away. Or one partner dies...

Jock thought back to the last time he'd seen his father, nearly fifteen years ago. Jock's father was a man who'd committed everything he had to his marriage. When his wife died, Sam Blaxton had been left with nothing but a hard, bitter shell, with no capacity to love at all.

He'd made his son's life hell.

Jock bit his lip and steered his little car out around the headland, enjoying the feel of the sea breeze against his face. He wanted none of it, the love bit. Marriage. Babies. He didn't want a bar of it.

This was what he wanted. Freedom. The wind in his face. The freedom to pick up his life and move on, as he would as soon as he had Tina and her tribe back on their feet again. How would it feel—to be as committed as Tina was to her family? He thought of the burden the girl was carrying and blenched inwardly. Debt. A sister totally dependent on her, and those three little lives...

Maybe it would have been better for Christie to abort the baby, he thought savagely. To bring another little life into this mess... Tina didn't have one baby too many to care for. She had a whole tribe too many. But then he thought back to Rose's perfect little face. Her red hair. The baby was going to have flaming hair, just like the others. Just like Tina's.

Hell, what was he thinking of?

Just get back to work, and start organising, he told himself savagely. The one thing he did not want was to involve himself emotionally, not now, not ever. He'd seen what lay down that road. All it led to was disaster.

Tina came back to work a week later. Jock didn't hear about it. He was suffering serious sleep deprivation after two nights awake, and the night of Tina's return he hit the pillow at seven p.m. At five in the morning she called him. Funny how a voice could get under your skin. Tina's voice, soft and melodic, sounded down the phone and it was like an extension of a dream.

'Jock?'

Jock had to shake himself to convince himself the voice was real. Tina calling to him through sleep was surely a dream. He lay on the pillows with the telephone receiver in his hand and thought really hankering thoughts about Tina.

'Jock?'

That woke him up. There was urgency in the way she spoke his name for the second time. He hauled himself back to being a doctor on call.

'I'm here, Tina!'

'Jock, I'm sorry,' she said, and her voice said she truly was sorry to have to wake him. 'But Mrs Blythe's just come in and we need you right away.'

Mrs Blythe...

Jock frowned. Julie Blythe was a young primigravida—a mum giving birth for the first time. He'd expect that if she'd just presented there'd be a long wait before delivery. It wasn't normal to call in the consultant as soon as a woman arrived in labour.

'Is there a problem?' He knew the answer before Tina spoke.

'Yes. Posterior presentation and she's waited too long to come in.'

'Posterior...'

'She really is in trouble, Jock. I think... Maybe a Caesarean, but she may have left it too late.'

'Ring Lloyd, then, and give him warning,' Jock snapped, his senses now fully tuned to medicine. If they had to do a Caesarean then they needed three doctors. He could do the delivery and Tina could do the anaesthetic but they needed another doctor for the baby.

'I don't know if a Caesarean's possible,' Tina faltered. 'Jock, hurry. I'm out of my depth here. This lady... She needs you now, Jock.'

So do I, Tina thought as she put the phone down and wondered how long it would take Jock to get to the hospital. So do I...

Jock was there in four minutes flat, breaking all legal limits and a few illegal ones to cover the half-mile trip from his beachfront house to the hospital. Tina's voice had been urgent and distressed, and he knew enough of Tina by now to respond. She wouldn't put that urgency into her voice if there wasn't a need.

One look at Mrs Blythe and he knew that Tina had been dead right when she'd made her voice urgent. It was the admitting officer's job to assess all patients as they arrived during the night. Jock's workload was too heavy to assume total care of patients through a long labour. The hospital was set up so that the admitting officer—casualty officer at night and thus Tina—checked the mothers as they arrived, did what had to be done and then called Jock as needed.

Tina had called Jock the moment she'd seen Julie Blythe, and then she'd sent the nursing staff to set up Theatre. He went to Labour Ward and was redirected to

Theatre—so Tina was still thinking Caesarean. He pushed through the swing doors of Theatre with a frown.

'What on earth…?' A posterior presentation didn't mean an automatic Caesarean, but Tina must have reasons for bringing Julie here. She did.

'Dr Blaxton, Mrs Blythe's been in labour for twenty-four hours,' Tina said, without looking up. She was setting up a drip, her face tight with strain. 'Mrs Blythe's husband was away and she didn't think the contractions were strong enough to worry about. Then, after her husband came home, things just got out of hand.'

'OK.' Jock walked swiftly over to the table and gave the frightened young mother's hand a reassuring squeeze. 'You have the full complement of labour staff here now, Mrs Blythe. Let's just see what this youngster of yours is doing.'

Julie Blythe was almost past responding. Her eyes were dulled with pain and she looked exhausted almost to death. As well she might. Two minutes later Jock's face was as strained as Tina's.

The baby was fully into the birth canal—as far down as it could go—but its posterior presentation meant that it could go no further. The relentless rhythmic contractions were causing swelling to the baby's head, meaning every moment the baby was in that position it was less likely to be born naturally. And it was so far down…

'I don't know if you can do a Caesar,' Tina said hesitantly. 'The baby's so close. But I thought…'

Her eyes flickered to the monitor. Leads ran from Julie's distended abdomen and the monitor showed how the baby was managing its fight for survival. It wasn't managing well. The heartbeat was faltering, and there was meconium staining adding to the overwhelming impression that whatever was to be done had to be done *fast*.

And Jock moved!

His orders came thick and fast, and Tina barely had time to be stunned. She'd expected a dead baby out of this. One look at this presentation and she'd almost given up hope. The imperative had to be to save Julie's life, but to get a live baby as well... Jock was going for it, and Tina followed orders with a gratitude that made her feel physically weak. Thank heaven for technical expertise. Thank heaven for specialists.

Thank heaven for Jock.

Under Jock's orders, Tina administered a pudendal block and then she watched as Jock's lubricated fingers carefully examined...felt the resistance, carefully probing for any room at all... Surely he couldn't deliver it normally, Tina thought, astounded. Surely...

'I want Kjelland's forceps,' Jock snapped, and then he was carefully adjusting the forceps...and then easing...forcing...the baby back, using all his strength and skill to rotate and push the baby back up the birth canal. Tina could only gaze in bewilderment as she followed Jock's snapped orders. She'd never seen this before. To push the baby back...

Whatever Jock was doing was working. The relentless contractions were easing, and Jock was pressing the baby away from the outside world.

'It's OK, Julie,' he murmured, through no one could know how much the young mother was taking in. 'We'll get this youngster out yet to meet his mama.' Jock didn't tell her that what he was doing was just the opposite to delivering a baby—forcing the child away from where it most wanted to be. 'You just hang in there...'

Then, to Tina, he added softly, 'Where's the father?'

'He's out in the waiting room. I thought...'

Jock nodded. He knew what Tina thought. Most obstetricians removed onlookers if things looked complicated. To work under this type of life-and-death stress was bad enough, but to work under stress with terrified

relatives watching was worse. But Julie Blythe was fading. Her breathing was rapid and shallow, and shock was
setting in.

'Sister, ask Mr Blythe to come in,' Jock said. 'Julie
needs all the support she can get here.'

A moment later a white-faced young man stumbled
into the room. He made it to his wife's side, gripped her
hand as if he were drowning and sat down hard on the
chair that the nurse provided. Tina had the overwhelming impression that he was sicker than his wife. Jock
waited until the young man was seated to speak to both
of them.

'We're going to perform a Caesarean section,' he told
them. 'Now.'

His eyes signalled his staff and Tina and the nurses
moved swiftly to set up screens across the woman's
breast and begin the process of anaesthetic block. Tina
was working on automatic pilot, following Jock blindly.
Had he moved the baby high enough to perform a
Caesarean? She wouldn't have thought so.

'Mr Blythe, I want you to support your wife,' Jock
was saying. 'Julie, can you hear me? Focus here, Mrs
Blythe. You're OK and we're nearly there. The baby
will be here soon, but we need to perform a Caesarean.
You know what that is. We make a small slit in your
tummy and lift the baby out. The baby's head's too
swollen to deliver normally. I'll deliver the baby now,
but I don't want to give you a general anaesthetic. I want
you to be wide awake to greet this baby.'

What Jock wasn't saying was that he was doubtful
whether Julie—or the baby—were in a fit condition to
cope with a general anaesthetic. Tina figured it out for
herself—and then blocked it out. She forced herself to
think solely about her anaesthetic skills. Only that. She
had to focus solely on her job and ignore the anxiety of
the young man and his wife.

'I think I might be sick. I...I don't know if I can stay,' the young man faltered, but Jock was having none of it.

'Julie has no choice and she needs you beside her,' Jock growled. 'Just hang on tight, and concentrate on caring for Julie. Talk her through this, Mr Blythe. You're all she has and she needs you.'

He turned to check monitors again.

'Lloyd's not here yet,' Tina told him. 'He was out at a call when I rang. Sally said he'd be here in ten minutes.'

All eyes were on those monitors. Jock's eyes narrowed. It was a risk to bring a baby into the world without another doctor ready to receive it to resuscitate if necessary. But another look at the monitors told him that the risks were worse if they waited. He gave Tina a grim, silent message with his eyes and Tina read the monitors and knew.

There was simply no time left at all. Those monitors had to keep up their message that this baby was still alive until Tina's anaesthetic could work, but that was all they could wait for. They must... And somehow they did. The anaesthetic took over. Jock waited until a last weak contraction passed—almost non-existent now. He checked the position of the baby's head once again— now as far back up the birth canal as he could get it— and then he took a deep, steadying breath—and cut.

Two minutes later a tiny sliver of a baby girl emerged to greet a new world, and after that suddenly everything was magically, wonderfully, OK again.

Lloyd burst in as the baby emerged, just in time. He cleared the baby's airway and checked the little one while Tina kept tabs on the anaesthetic and Jock stitched the wound. By the time Jock put in the first stitch their new arrival was wailing her lungs out. Lloyd was hardly needed.

'Is this all you kept me out of bed for?' he demanded,

but his eyes twinkled. Lloyd had babies of his own and Lloyd loved babies. He wasn't a paediatrician, he was a physician, but he was thoroughly enjoying looking after Gina's paediatric practice while she and Struan were away.

'One healthy baby? One gorgeous little girl?' Lloyd beamed at both parents. 'Congratulations to the pair of you, but I'm back to bed. Your daughter doesn't need a doctor and I only have an hour or so before my tribe wake up.' The physician grinned at Jock and Tina, sketched them a mock salute and took himself back to bed.

Jock finished his suturing and turned to check what Tina was doing.

'I want two million units of penicillin in that drip,' he told Tina, and she looked up from adjusting the drip stand and stared.

'Two million...' She frowned. 'Surely not. It was a straightforward Caesar—'

'Two million,' Jock snapped, and there was a sudden tense silence in the room.

'OK.' Tina shrugged. She hadn't meant to query him. It wasn't her place as anaesthetist to question the obstetrician, but the dosage was certainly high. It couldn't do any harm, though. It would certainly stop any hint of infection in its tracks, and the tension cleared again. With the drip adjusted, the orderly wheeled Julie off to Maternity, her husband following her trolley like a puffed-up lion. Bill Blythe had grown a full six inches with the advent of fatherhood. Ellen took the baby off to the nursery to be washed and dressed, and Jock and Tina were left alone.

CHAPTER FOUR

ALL of a sudden the silence was deafening. Awkward even. There was a tenseness between them that Tina couldn't fathom. It was as if there was a frisson, running back and forth. An electric current that had nowhere to go except between their two bodies.

'I'm sorry about the antibiotic,' Tina said awkwardly. 'I didn't mean to question you. It's just that it's not the usual dose.'

'I like to be sure,' replied Jock.

'I guess...'

It had been the dosage Tina would have given if the Caesar had been done in less than aseptic conditions, though. There had to be a reason for it. Still... Hers not to reason why. She was the junior doctor here, and Jock's obstetric skills were certainly not in question.

'I guess you should go back to bed, too,' Tina said slowly as she crossed to the sink. 'I'm sorry I had to wake you.'

Jock's frown cleared. 'Don't be sorry. It's worth waking to get a result like this.'

'If she'd left it any longer she could have died. And the baby almost did.'

'Yes.'

Both of them fell silent, knowing just how close they'd come to the edge. If Jock hadn't been so skilled...

'I wasn't expecting you to be back at work so soon,' Jock said brusquely, shoving unwelcome scenarios aside. 'I thought Sally was looking after the hospital tonight.'

'She was, but we arrived back from Sydney yesterday

in time for me to attend Mary's kitchen tea—I'm chief bridesmaid, you know, so I have an obligation. Then I rang in and said I'd take over for the night.' Tina gave a prim little smile. 'Christie's come back with me, and Marie's every bit as competent as you promised in looking after Christie and the children. So I'm back. I like to carry my own workload, Dr Blaxton.'

'I can see that.' Jock hauled off his theatre gown and hurled it down the laundry chute with more force than was necessary. The gesture helped get rid of some of the damned electricity he was feeling. Electricity? Whatever it was. Whatever... 'How's your sister?'

'Better.'

'Define better.'

'She's not at death's door any more,' Tina said, and Jock looked up from turning on the taps, startled.

'Was she ever? Isn't that being a bit melodramatic?'

'Meaning she wasn't at death's door when she went to Sydney?' Tina shrugged. 'I think she was. She'd stopped eating. Things were way out of control.' Tina took a deep breath. 'The real reason I insisted on her being admitted to a psychiatric hospital was that she needed medical care but I was afraid of suicide.'

'And now?'

'Now she's eating again. She's rested. She's talking sense. So it's up to me...to me and the kids to bring her back, and we will.'

Jock's frown deepened. 'If she really was that bad, then it'll take months.'

'I know that. I have months.'

Jock's eyebrows furrowed, concerned. 'But what about your own life during these months?' he asked gently, watching Tina's face as he washed the talcum from his ungloved hands. 'Tell me. What were you doing in Brisbane when you dropped everything to come here?'

'You already know some of it,' Tina said doubtfully. It was weird, standing at the sinks beside this man. Weirdly intimate. She'd spent heaps of time in operating theatres in her medical career, but with Jock it was a whole new feeling. Weird! She took a long, slow breath, trying to sort sense from her jumbled thoughts. 'I imagine you saw what I've done from reading my résumé when I applied for the job here.'

Jock nodded, remembering Tina's curriculum vitae. 'I remember. You'd just finished your first part anaesthetics—for which Julie Blythe, Bill Blythe, young Blythe junior and I are profoundly grateful. That was a skilled anaesthetic job you did there.' Ignoring Tina's flush of pleasure, he kept right on probing. 'So you hadn't found a registrar position for your anaesthetic second part?'

'I... Yes, I had, but—'

'But you abandoned your plans—and your job—to come here.' Jock nodded. 'That's what I thought. With the skills you have, finding a registrar job would be no problem. But to give it up... That means a year out of your career plans. The registrar jobs don't come up again until early next year.'

'Someone might drop out and create a vacancy.' That's what Tina had told herself. She'd agonised for a whole two minutes about giving up her job. There hadn't been a choice, but she'd known what she was losing. 'I might be lucky.'

'But you might not.' Jock looked at her curiously across the sinks. 'And how about your social life? Do you have a boyfriend?'

Tina flushed again. Drat the man, he really had the power to unsettle her. 'That's none of your business.'

But Jock was reading her face and to Tina's disgust he did it with ease. 'So there is someone waiting patiently in the wings?'

Tina thought of Peter, waiting patiently back in

Sydney. That was exactly how she'd describe him. Peter waiting patiently in the wings for some spark to ignite between them. She and Peter suited each other—they had heaps in common but maybe not enough for marriage, and both of them knew it. Peter was a sweetheart, a patient sweetheart. It was a pity he was a sweetheart who didn't make her toes curl.

'If you must know, I do have a boyfriend,' she said, and she couldn't make her voice sound the way she wanted. She was willing her voice to sound warm, definite and sure. Instead, all she sounded was defensive. 'His name's Peter.'

'Peter's another doctor?'

'He's a surgeon.'

'Bully for Peter.' Jock's voice wasn't quite under control either. There was a growl of anger underneath that neither he nor Tina understood. 'Is he coming to see you next weekend?'

'No.' Tina flashed Jock a startled glance. 'Why should he?'

'Did you see him in Sydney?'

Good grief! Tina glowered and backed away from the sinks. 'Of course I did. What is this, Dr Blaxton? A private grilling? Me and Peter—'

'You and your Peter are nothing to do with me,' Jock agreed, and he flashed out his smile again. The smile that had Tina's toes doing the sorts of things she wished Peter could make them do. 'I know it's none of my business,' he added. 'It's just…'

Then Jock hesitated, as if he was suddenly about to do something that might not be wise. Then he shrugged. 'Tina, the hospital dance is on Saturday night. I need someone to come with me.'

Tina's eyebrows rose. Her stomach was turning somersaults and so were her toes, but she managed to keep her face straight. 'Really?'

'Really.'

'Well, I can't see the problem. I imagine there'll be a queue,' she managed dryly.

'What's that supposed to mean?'

'Meaning, according to the nursing staff, finding a date has never been a problem for you.'

It was Jock's turn to raise his eyebrows. 'Tina, are you accusing me of being a playboy?'

Tina considered. 'Yes,' she said at last, and managed a grin. 'I've heard that's exactly what you are. According to the nurses, you never take anyone out more than twice.'

'Is that a problem for you?'

'Oh, not for me, it's not,' Tina said cheerfully. 'But, then, I'm not in the market for a long-term relationship.'

'Because you have one with Peter.'

'Because I have one with Peter,' she agreed flatly, trying to ignore the weird sensation still coursing round in her toes. 'What's your excuse?' As she watched Jock's face, Tina frowned. 'There really is a reason, isn't there, Dr Blaxton? There's a reason you don't take women out more than twice.'

'I...'

'You're not gay, are you?'

Jock stared, and then he choked.

'No, Dr Rafter, I am *not* gay. Do I seem gay?'

'N-no.' She looked sideways up at him and managed a grin. Good grief! Masculinity—sheer arrant sex appeal—oozed out of every pore of this man. 'I guess not.'

'*You guess...*'

That got her laughing out loud. There was no way she could keep a straight face before his incredulity. 'No.' Then, at the look of Jock's affronted face—and as he took two threatening steps toward her—she held up wet hands to fend him off. 'OK. I know you're not. But...'

'But what?'

'Why don't you take women out more than twice?'

That was easy. 'They fall in love with me,' he complained.

'Oh.' Tina grinned. 'Silly me. Now why didn't I think of that for an answer?'

'You're laughing at me.'

'Yep.'

'Dr Rafter...'

She backed another step. 'You don't think you just might sound a touch conceited here?'

It was Jock's turn to smile then. 'I guess I do at that,' he conceded. 'I'm sorry. I'm just not in the market for "serious".'

Tina considered. 'So what's so appalling about someone getting serious?' she demanded. 'You might just like it.'

'Nope.'

'That's very definite.'

'It is.'

Tina's laughter died as she heard the note of gravity beneath his words. 'Do you want to tell me why?'

Jock's laughter faded as well.

'Let's just say I don't wish to share the experience.' He shrugged. 'However... Seeing you're nicely settled with your Peter, but your Peter's in Sydney... Seeing you're not in the market for a long-term relationship... How do you feel about coming to the dance with me on Saturday night?'

He smiled again, and Tina's heart did a backward somersault. Which it had no business doing, she thought crossly, not with Peter waiting patiently in the wings. So what should she do here? Ignore the somersaults? Ignore the curling toes?

If she *could* ignore them then maybe it would be fun, Tina thought. Life had been altogether too serious for too long now, and Christie was feeling guilty about Tina being here. Apart from Mary's kitchen tea, Tina had had no social life at all since she'd returned here to live. With Marie living in, there was nothing to stop her enjoying herself now. If Christie could see that she was getting out…having fun… It would be fun to go out with Jock.

Jock Blaxton… He was smiling at her, waiting for an answer, and his eyes were dark and kind and warm. Involuntarily, Tina's toes did their curling bit again and she struggled to straighten them. For heaven's sake—what was happening here? Keep it light, keep it casual!

'Well…' Tina's face grew thoughtful. How to keep this as casual as possible… 'Maybe. But…'

'But?'

Jock was using her, Tina decided, using her as a date to serve his own ends. So she could use him just the same.

'The dance is an after-dinner affair,' she said thoughtfully. 'So… I'll be your date for the dance if you come and have a picnic first with Christie and the children and me.'

'What, out at the cottage?' he asked, startled.

'Yep.' She grinned. It was time Christie had a bit of company—time she saw other people—and Tina knew Jock well enough to know he'd be empathic. 'If I work every night until then, I'll be off duty from Friday. So Saturday afternoon I'll be raring to go, and so will the children. There's a big dam out behind the ridge. Bring your bathers, we'll take the children for a swim, have tea and then come in to the dance.'

'Take the children…'

'You don't mind a bit of domesticity, do you?' Tina asked demurely. 'Or is that what you're running from, Jock?'

'No.' Jock shook his head and smiled. 'I don't mind a bit of domesticity. As long as it's not my own.'

'That's OK, then.' Tina smiled straight back at him,

ignoring the odd lurch in her innards. 'We have a date. I'll see you on Saturday. About four?'

'About four. I'll look forward to it.'

But suddenly Jock wasn't sure whether he was looking forward to it or not. The same old fear reached out to clutch him. Usually it was after the first couple of dates that he felt like this, like running a mile. But now... With this girl the fear was striking early. Tina was *not* interested in him, he told himself savagely. *Not!* She had a life to lead. As soon as she had her sister back on her feet she'd be off back to Sydney. Off to her boyfriend. There was no risk to him to take her out. So why did he feel as if his foundations were shifting from under him?

'Babies permitting,' he reminded her, and suddenly he thought that babies might be just what was called for here. He needed a good long labour next Saturday afternoon to get him out of this swim and dinner. Then he needed to free a couple of hours to collect Tina and make his token appearance at the dance. Then he needed another labour to follow.

That's what he needed. It was unfortunate that he couldn't make babies come on demand.

'I hope you don't get a baby, then,' Tina said lightly—and Jock could only agree with her.

'I don't know about you going to this dance with Jock.'

Tina was in the nursery with Ellen, before going off duty. Tina hadn't been able to resist having a last look at young Laura Blythe. Two hours old and already making her presence felt from one end of the hospital to the other, Laura was *some* baby. She was gorgeous. Unable to resist, Tina lifted her out of her cot and cuddled her close.

'Listen you, your mummy's asleep. You give her a

couple of hours' grace before you start demanding tucker.'

The baby gave an indignant wuffle and snuggled her face into Tina's breast. Two hours old and she already knew exactly what she wanted. No wonder she'd survived. This little one had taken a huge battering. She was a survivor in anyone's books.

'You like babies, don't you?' Ellen said softly, and Tina smiled.

'Isn't it obvious?'

'You'd like to have your own one day?'

'Well, of course.'

'I don't think Dr Blaxton does.'

'No?' Tina cradled the little one closer, trying not to be too interested. There was no reason for her to be interested—was there? 'He likes babies, though.'

'He does.' Ellen compressed her lips in disapproval. 'He likes them from a distance—but not for keeps. He's not in the market for a long-term relationship. Anyone can see that.'

'Well, neither am I,' Tina managed lightly. 'So we should suit.'

'That's what all my nurses say before they go out with him.' Ellen sniffed. 'One after the other, I see 'em go out. One date is all it takes with *that* man. They come back with stars in their eyes. After the second date they come back and their feet don't touch the floor. Then he asks someone else out and they howl for a month—or pine, which is worse. I've had so many lovesick nurses...'

'Surely not,' Tina said, startled. 'For heaven's sake, Ellen... You make him sound like James Bond without the gun.'

'Yeah. Maybe it's a good comparison. Move over, Sean Connery.'

Tina giggled. 'It doesn't fit. His car doesn't have as many gadgets.'

'No.' But Ellen didn't giggle, and even her smile faded as she watched her young friend.

'Ellen...'

'All I'm saying is be careful,' Ellen said sternly. 'You're young and impressionable...'

'I'm twenty-eight, for heaven's sake. Nearly twenty-nine.'

'Then you're mature and impressionable. But Jock is dangerous, Tina. You mark my words.'

'Ellen, I'm going to the dance with him. That's all. I'm not about to fall for a pretty face.'

'If I thought Jock was just a pretty face I shouldn't worry.'

'Then what are you worrying about?' Tina fixed her friend with a look. 'For heaven's sake, Ellen, just what is worrying you about Jock?'

'He has ghosts.' Ellen grimaced. 'And the ghosts hurt him and everyone around him.'

'Ghosts?' Tina smiled, refusing to match Ellen's grimness. 'What sort of ghosts?'

'His mother's ghost for one. There may be more. But I doubt if any girl will get close to him. Ever.'

'So...how come Dr Blaxton has his mother's ghost tagging along for the ride?' Keep it light, Tina told herself. Keep it light, even though you desperately want to know.

Ellen shrugged. She hardly spoke of Jock's mother now. She hardly even thought of the woman who'd once been her best friend. The pain from years ago had faded. It was only when she looked at Jock's face...saw the traces of pain still lingering there...that she remembered.

'Jock's mother had an emergency Caesarean to give birth to Jock,' she said softly. 'She wasn't well looked after. She had a huge pelvic infection.'

'I see.' Tina nodded, thinking of Jock's attitude to Julie's antibiotics. 'I can understand that.'

'I'm not sure that you do,' Ellen said sadly. 'The infection didn't disappear without damage, but caused adhesions. Jock's mother needed operation after operation to correct the problems, but each operation made things worse. She was in and out of hospital for the rest of her life. She wasn't able to have more children, and she was in constant pain. The adhesions got worse and worse—and finally when Jock was ten years old they caused a complete bowel obstruction. She died just before Jock's eleventh birthday.'

'Oh, no...'

'There's worse,' Ellen said grimly. 'All of us...all of Jock's mother's friends... We wanted to help Jock so much. But Jock's father was a hard, unforgiving man. He loved his wife very much, loved her past reason. I think...watching her die, he went a little bit crazy. If she had to die, then someone had to be to blame.'

'Not Jock.'

'Jock.' Ellen closed her eyes, remembering past pain. The pain was all around her again. How could she have thought she could forget? 'Yes, Jock. Sam Blaxton blamed his son totally for his wife's death. According to Sam, they'd had one baby and that baby was one baby too many. Jock should never have been born and he was never allowed to forget it.'

'Oh, Ellen...'

'So you keep a hold on your heart when you're around Jock, my girl,' Ellen went on grimly, 'because, charming as Jock is, there are some wounds that can't be healed. He's grown up thinking that there are too many babies in the world. It's been drilled into him that even his own birth was a mistake. He's an obstetrician, and I'll bet part of the reason for his career choice was to ensure what happened to his mother doesn't happen to anyone else. But I can't ever see him having babies of his own. Can you?'

Jock arrived at Christie's farm right on the dot of four o'clock on Saturday. No babies arrived to hold him up, and when he saw Ally and Tim, hanging over the verandah rails, he couldn't be sorry he'd arrived in time to take them for a swim. Nor could he regret it when Tina came out the front door, wearing a scanty yellow bikini and a baby pouch, and nothing more.

The sight of Tina acted like a hard kick in the guts, he thought breathlessly. She looked stunning, standing behind the verandah railings, practically naked, but with a tiny baby pouch cradled against her naked skin...

Whew...

'Hi!' Tina came lightly down the steps toward him, the baby bouncing happily before her, and the kicked feeling in his gut only got worse. He was finding it hard to breathe.

'Hi.' Jock managed to make his voice normal—but only just. He checked her out from the toes up, but closer inspection only got better. He was starting to feel like he needed a ventilator. 'Are we all going swimming, then?' he managed. 'Even Rose?'

'Silly. Rose can't swim yet.' It was four-year-old Ally, swooping down on Jock's car and dragging Tim behind her. 'Rose's staying with Mummy. Will you drive us to the dam in your car?'

'Ally, we'll walk,' Tina said, laughing. 'This little car can't drive over paddocks.' Her voice made it quite clear what she thought of Jock's ridiculous car.

'It will so,' Jock said, offended. 'It doesn't mind the odd bump.'

'What about tree stumps?'

'It's good at dodging.'

'There are only two seats.'

'If we're not going out onto the road, then we can all squash.'

'Oh, yeah? And come back all muddy, and squish our mud down on your leather upholstery...'

Jock glared. It was as if Tina was finding malicious enjoyment in telling him how unsuitable his car was, and Jock rose right to the bait.

'My leather will wash.'

'Are you sure?'

'Yes!'

'Well, that's great, then.' Tina gave Jock a grin of unholy amusement, and she swung Tim's small body up and plonked him in the passenger side. 'Great. You're right, Dr Blaxton. It's really too far to walk, but I don't want to get *my* car full of mud so it's very nice of you to offer your car's services.'

Then, as Jock choked in indignant laughter, Tina looked back at the house—to see a woman emerge from the front door. Jock's gaze followed hers. This must be Christie. It had to be Christie. The woman was a pale, frail echo of Tina. Same vibrant colouring—same flame-coloured hair—but on Christie the colouring looked all wrong. As if her body wasn't strong enough to support it.

Christie was painfully thin, and the hand which clung to the verandah rail had skin stretched tight and was blue-veined from emaciation. She was dressed, simply, in a cotton frock which hung on her too thin body, but Jock knew how much effort it cost severely depressed people to dress. Dressing was a sign of recovery. Christie's hair had been brushed until it shone and she was managing a tremulous smile.

'So this is your Dr Blaxton, Tina.'

'He's not my Dr Blaxton.' Tina swung her lithe body up the steps to her sister and stood beside her, gazing down at Jock. Her eyes were still twinkling mischief. 'I

have him for two dates. He only ever concedes two in-
vitations to each of his lucky ladies. Then he's off to the
next conquest. So it's up to me to get as much as I can
out of him on each visit.'

'Tina!' Christie sounded shocked, but she kept up her
smile as Jock unwound his long body from the car and
strode up the verandah to meet her. 'You'll have to excuse Tina,' she told Jock in a voice that wasn't quite
steady. 'She was brought up badly.'

'I was not!' Tina grinned. 'I just have bad genes.
Christie did what she could with me, but you can't make
a silk purse out of a sow's ear, no matter how you try.'

Both sisters chuckled and Jock looked from Tina to
Christie in astonishment. Tina was gorgeous. Tina and
Christie were both gorgeous. They were all gorgeous,
Jock thought desperately, looking around at this little
family. They were embedded in poverty up to their ears,
Christie was ill, they were fighting to stay afloat and yet
they could still laugh.

Christie. Concentrate on Christie, he told himself. And
block out the thought of Tina's long bare legs right there
beside you!

Jock took Christie's fragile hand in his, held it hard,
and concentrated. 'Hello, Mrs Maiden. I'm so glad I'm
finally meeting you. I'm glad that I'm finally able to say
I'm sorry I wasn't here to look after you when you had
Rose.' His smile reached out to this frail woman and
held her. 'I'm so sorry my locum treated you as he did,'
he added gently. 'I have a lot to apologise for.'

'But…it wasn't your fault,' Christie said faintly. 'The
whole thing was my fault. Tina said I should have been
seeing you all through my pregnancy and you never
would have let me get in this state. I know she's right,
but—'

'But sometimes depression is a downward spiral, with
relentless pressure keeping you down,' Jock said softly.

'There's no way you can climb out of it without help. I know. You were in shock and then you copped postnatal depression on top of it. Postnatal depression is a physical illness. It's an imbalance of hormones that we don't fully understand yet. That meant you had physical illness on top of mental strain. It's a wonder you didn't go all the way under—and yet here you are, smiling!'

'Tina makes me smile,' Christie said simply, and Jock nodded, and looked down at Tina's legs. Yeah!

'Tina would make anyone smile.'

'Does that mean I'm a joke?' Tina said huffily, hoisting Rose higher against her breast. 'Hey, Rose, do you hear that? They're accusing your Aunty Tina of being a clown.'

But Jock was back concentrating on Christie, avoiding Tina's bare toes.

'Mrs Maiden, now you're home…now you've got child care…'

'Thanks to you,' Christie told him.

'Providing child care is the least I can do after my locum's cavalier treatment of you,' Jock said bluntly. 'You're not to feel grateful. Paying Marie gets me off the hook, guiltwise. But for the rest… You're not to stop treatment now that you're home from hospital. Would you let me see you professionally?'

He heard Tina's sharp intake of breath beside him but she didn't say a word. Nothing. The whole world seemed to hang on Christie's answer.

'I don't know,' Christie said dubiously, looking up into Jock's face with doubt. 'I don't really need a—'

'You don't trust doctors,' Jock finished for her, deliberately twisting her irresolution. 'Given your experience with Henry—with my locum—I don't blame you. But I would ask for you to trust just one more time. Come and see me.'

Jock's smile was gentle—beguiling—and beside him

Tina held her breath. He lifted a notebook from his shirt pocket and flipped open its pages. 'What about Monday morning at eleven a.m.? Can you see me then? Marie could bring you in. Would you trust me that much, Mrs Maiden?'

'My name's Christie,' Christie said blankly, and Jock's smile broadened. He kept his eyes on hers, refusing to break the moment.

'Christie, then. Do you trust me?' Then he motioned to where Ally and Tim were piling water-wings, a rubber duck and various floaties into his car. 'You're trusting me to take care of Ally and Tim and Tina. How about yourself?'

'I don't—'

'Christie, please. I'm going to feel bad for the rest of my life if you don't let me help.'

Christie stared, and finally that shy, tentative smile peeped out again—an echo of Tina's smile. The promise of what might come again. 'Oh, heck... I can see why Tina says you're dangerous, Dr Blaxton,' she said softly. 'You could talk blood out of stone. Very well. I'll come in and see you on Monday morning.'

Jock caught both her hands and his smile lit his whole face.

'Hey, Christie, that's great,' he said. 'With me looking after you medically, with Tina bludgeoning you domestically, with Marie to help with the kids and with your inner strength we'll conquer this damned depression. You just see if we don't!'

'I don't think this damned depression stands a chance,' Christie said faintly. 'Not with you and Tina working on it. You two make a powerful team! You take my breath away.'

CHAPTER FIVE

'YOU were great.'

Squashed beneath children, water-wings and a vast beach-ball, it was all Tina could do to make herself heard as they bounced across the paddocks, but somehow she did and Jock grinned. This wasn't his normal sort of date, he decided. Once he'd seen Tina in her gorgeous bikini, he very much fancied having her beside him in his little car. He didn't even mind Rose cradled against her breast. But they'd left Rose with Christie.

'Marie will be here in an hour and it does Christie good to have time alone with her baby—I wanted her to come with us but she's not quite ready for that,' Tina had told him. She had organised everyone else into the car and now Jock couldn't even *see* Tina, much less appreciate her gorgeous body. But he could react to the warmth in her voice.

'How do you mean—I was great?' he asked cautiously. 'And you used the past tense. Does that mean that once I was great but now I'm a poor squirming excuse for an obstetrician and gynaecologist?'

'I meant with Christie.' Tina grinned herself and wriggled happily under a couple of squirmy bodies. Ally and Tim were holding onto the windscreen and bouncing up and down on her lap with excitement. 'How did you know she's still reluctant to see doctors?'

'I guessed. Do you think she'll come and see me?'

'Now she has a definite appointment and she's met you, she'll come. The hard part's over.' Tina's smile faded and she sighed. 'I just wish... I wish you'd been here for her when she had Rose. I wish I'd been here.'

'Don't think about it,' Jock said gently. 'We're here now. She has all the support she needs and she'll make it. She's on the other side of the abyss now, Tina.'

'Maybe.'

'She must be.' Jock steered around a tree stump and the little car bounced. 'Who's the psychiatrist who looked after her in Sydney?'

Tina told him and Jock nodded with recognition.

'She's great. If Pat Morgan said Christie's OK to come home then she's OK to come home. She wouldn't let her out of her sight if she didn't think she was recovering.'

'Yeah, well, I still want to thank you,' Tina told him, her voice distant and pensive. 'After all the bad-mouthing I did... You really were...well...great!'

The word echoed on the breeze and Jock gave himself a fast mental shake. For Tina to give him such praise when he hadn't earned it... How on earth was it possible for one slip of a girl to get under his skin like she did?

Keep it light.

'Well, what did you expect?' he demanded. He made the words smug, shoving away sensations he didn't know how to deal with and concentrating fiercely on humour. 'Great is in the job description of medical specialists,' he told her, chuckling. 'You wait. The minute you qualify as an anaesthetist you'll be great, too. The only people greater are surgeons. You call them mister and you practically have to tug a forelock every time they glide their imperial presences into your orbit.'

Tina chuckled with him, the tension eased and they set about enjoying their afternoon, which they did. They all did. The dam was just under the rise to the mountains beyond the coastal plains. It was a tiny hollow, forming a catchment for the crystal clear mountain run-off. Vast gums towered overhead, and at some stage—millions of years ago—this whole coastal plain must have all been under the sea. The remnant still remained. Magically, the north end of the dam was a sandy beach, with soft white sand and a littering of ancient sea shells.

Jock stopped his little car just before the sand and gazed in awe.

'Wow!'

'It is wow, isn't it?' Tina said softly, and then she flung open her car door and gave an Indian war whoop in glee. 'OK, kids. Last one in the water is a one-legged yabby. Let's go.'

Her bubble of excitement lasted all afternoon. Jock lay on his back and floated in the sun-warmed water, shaded from sunburn by the canopy of the vast gum trees and content to watch Tina playing with her niece and nephew.

She let him be, and that, in itself, was a novelty. Most girls Jock Blaxton dated were all over him. They'd never let their attention be deflected by two small children.

Tina was different.

He'd never met anyone like this, he thought, wondering, as he watched her. Tina took life in both hands and she wrung every last ounce of enjoyment from it. She held these two little children in thrall, towing them around the dam in their water-wings, diving under them and coming up as a 'Tina shark'. Laughing, always laughing.

She served out a picnic tea she'd made that morning and got more cream on her nose from her cream cakes than either of the children did, not being the least embarrassed when Jock pointed out her creamy nose. In fact, Tina promptly turned it into a competition, daubing each of their noses with cream and seeing who could make the best job of licking it off.

She even had Jock stretching his tongue out as far as he could, joining in their ridiculous game with the children and Tina yelling encouragement as he finally reached the offending cream.

'Jock's got the biggest tongue. Jock's got the biggest tongue,' the children yelled, as Tina convulsed in laughter. Then Tina tried the same trick—and her tongue neatly reached up and removed her cream in one dextrous swipe.

The children were spellbound.

'You've been practising,' Jock said accusingly, and Tina gave him a bland smile.

'Yep. All my life. It's my one claim to fame and now it's finally paid off. I'm not a medical specialist yet, but I'm more great than you are at cream-licking, Jock Blaxton. Beat that, Mr Specialist!' Then she grabbed a child in each hand and whirled them around back into the water. 'OK, kids. One more lap of the dam to de-icecream and then it's time for me and Jock to dress up and head for the dance.'

Her lovely, lithe body knifed down into the water, with the children tumbling after, and Jock was left staring after her as if he'd been struck dumb. Good grief! He didn't follow. He couldn't. His body seemed overcome by inertia—or was it that he just didn't trust himself to join her? To be near that lovely, near-naked body...

So Jock lay in the sunlight on the soft sand and stared at her in amazement as she played with her niece and nephew, trying to figure out what he was feeling. What was happening to him here? This was a crazy, out-of-body experience. This girl... It was the setting, he told himself savagely. Only the setting. This must be one of the loveliest places in the world. But it wasn't the setting, it was Tina.

Hell!

Jock looked out over the water and watched as Tina towed her two little charges around the dam. She was floating on her back, her feet kicking her on strongly, and she had ropes attached to her wrists and then to a child apiece. The children were laughing and whooping and Tina was laughing and whooping right back. They were a lovely, laughing family. What would it be like? To have a family like this of his own?

Oh, yeah, sure! What was he thinking? Jock gave himself a harsh mental shake. One beautiful setting, one gorgeous girl and a couple of nice kids, and all of a sudden everything he'd promised himself for the last twenty years looked like being thrown out the window. No way. Jock let his thoughts drift back to his father. To the overwhelming bitterness his father had carried to the grave.

'You let your heart go once and you're stuffed for life,' his father had told him over and over. 'I wish I'd never met your mother. I fell for her and that was that. Nine months… Nine months of pregnancy and then ten years watching her die. And then having to see you every day of my life… See you in her…'

The bitterness had been all around them. It would stay with Jock for ever.

'If you fall for a woman then you're a fool,' his father had told him. 'You're not in control for the rest of your life. It's a hard lesson, boy, but if I can teach you that then it'll be a lesson well learned. Don't lose control. Not ever…'

Jock looked over the water, and he knew for the first time what his father had been trying to tell him. Because for the first time in his life he felt totally out of control.

The feeling grew worse. They took the children back to the house and showered and changed for the dance. Jock took first shower and then chatted easily to Christie, Marie and the children while he waited for Tina. He lifted Rose from her crib and played with her—hey, she was smiling already—and the time flew. And to Jock's astonishment Tina took only fifteen minutes.

Fifteen minutes to be ready for a dance! Jock had resigned himself to wait for an hour. As she came out the bedroom door he stared in incredulity. And kept on staring.

'What's wrong?' Tina smiled across the room at him, her laughing eyes mocking. She twirled. 'Is my dress too short?'

Too short!

It was short, Jock acknowledged. It was tiny. It was a tiny wisp of crimson, with pencil-slim shoulder straps, a plunging neckline front and back, figure-hugging form at the waist and then a skirt that flared softly out around her thighs. Soft silk, diaphanous folds which ended just below her...just below...

Jock swallowed.

Just below her hips. Just! And her legs... Tina was all legs and they were *some* legs! She was wearing shimmering silver stockings that showed her beautifully curved thighs and calves to perfection. She wore high, high stilettos and she looked... She looked a million dollars.

'Your hair's still wet,' Marie said blandly. The middle-aged mothercraft nurse was watching Jock's face with interest. 'You'll catch your death!'

'It takes ages to blow-dry and it'll dry by itself in Jock's car,' Tina retorted. 'If he leaves the roof down.' Tina swung her mass of damp curls around her shoulders and smiled down at Jock. 'Does your little car have hair-drying in its job description?'

Gorgeous! She was gorgeous! Jock cleared his throat and rose from where he'd been sitting at the table with Christie and Marie. He didn't look too bad himself, Tina thought as she watched him rise. In fact... In his deep black dinner suit Jock looked downright stunning. Smashing! And holding Rose in his arms... He looked so right. he was so good with babies! What a waste that he wouldn't consider one of his own.

He was born husband material. Born lover material!

Whoa... Where were her thoughts leading her? Tina couldn't afford to think what she was thinking, she told herself severely, because this was her first date with this man and after the second date there was nothing more. She knew that. She'd heard it from everyone, Jock included. She could still think he was good-looking, she told herself. Just...just not that he was desirable.

'Tina, do you think that dress is short enough?' Christie was asking dryly. 'You don't think you should hitch it up a bit at the shoulders?'

'It'll be a shirt if I do.' Tina chuckled. 'It's only just hiding my knickers as it is.'

The wind was right out of Jock's lungs. He was finding it harder and harder to breathe. Marie and Christie were watching his face and he was finding it harder and harder to keep an expression on his face which wasn't completely facile. He felt like a fawning Labrador puppy, dearly wanting to wag his tail.

'You want to leave now?' Tina glanced down at her wrist-watch—the only piece of jewellery she'd allowed herself on her creamy skin. 'It's seven-thirty. Hand Rose back to her mother and let's go, Dr Blaxton, while that bleeper of yours stays silent. We don't know how long we have before another baby comes along. So let's enjoy what time we have.'

Jock thought fleetingly back to his wish that he be called out tonight to a couple of complicated deliveries. If he was called now, he'd slit his throat, he thought. Tina was coming to the hospital dance as his partner— *his partner*—and the thought took his breath away.

The dance was wonderful.

Tina enjoyed herself immensely, but afterwards Jock

could remember only snatches. Snatches of memory, such as his colleague, Lloyd Neale, meeting Tina for the first time out of her doctor's uniform and staring at her as if he'd been struck as dumb as Jock. And Sally coming up and tucking her hand possessively in her husband's arm.

'You're a happily married man, Lloyd Neale so you can take your eyes off Tina's dress—or rather, lack of dress—and leave her to Jock.' Then Sally, gorgeous herself in a soft cream dress that suited her figure to perfection, smiled happily at Tina. 'Though I'd think something was wrong with my Lloyd if he didn't look. You look fabulous, Tina. Take her away, Jock, and hold her close or we'll have to put blinkers on every other man in the room.'

So Jock did just that. He whirled Tina onto the dance floor and placed his hands on her slim, compliant waist and drew her in to him... The room spinning... Being tapped on the shoulder more times than he cared to remember.

'Give over, Doc. Doc Rafter's a single lady. Give us a turn.'

The local bachelors vying with each other for Tina's attention and vying with Jock.

'Don't you devote yourself solely to Doc Blaxton, Doc Rafter. You remember me? I used to borrow your pencils way back in grade three. If I'd known you were going to turn out like this, Tina Rafter, I'd have given you all my pencils, no sweat. Give us a dance, Doc, and we'll talk about how many ways I can pay you back.'

Tina smiling and laughing, tossing that glorious hair and letting her own slim hands hold firmly onto Jock.

'Not tonight, guys. I'm partnering Dr Blaxton until his next baby comes along. Leave us alone!'

How could Jock have wanted a baby to intrude on tonight? But, of course, he got one. About midnight, just as the music started to slow and the dancers moved closer—and Jock's senses were starting to swim way off to some distant point in a tropical horizon—the tiny electronic buzzer at Jock's waist chirped into life.

'Hell.' Jock hauled himself back to reality with a huge mental effort. He drew back from Tina, flicked open his pager and swore again.

'I need to find a phone,' he told her. 'Sam Hopper's on call tonight but this message says he wants me to call him. Hopefully he just needs some advice. Will you wait for me?'

Famous last words. Wait! Jock had gone no more than two feet from Tina's side before she was whisked away in the arms of Kevin Blewitt, the local pharmacist.

I want to be a pharmacist, Jock thought bitterly as he searched for a phone. Nice regular hours. A shop I can shut at six o'clock and go home...

He swore again. How he was going to retrieve Tina after the phone call? The pharmacist was already holding Tina closer than Jock liked. But there was no call for him to retrieve Tina from her pharmacist's hold. Sam Hopper, one of the town's general practitioners, was terse and anxious and Jock just had to listen to the man's voice to know he'd be needed.

'Jock, I'm sorry, mate, but I've had a prolapse.'

A prolapse...

Jock closed his eyes. Hell!

This was a hard call. Sam was a general practitioner who insisted on doing his own deliveries. There were competent general practitioners in the district who delivered their own babies, but Sam wasn't one of them. First, he had a tiny practice and he only delivered five or six babies a year. That meant that he simply didn't have a wide enough experience to keep his hand in.

Second, the man was arrogant and he loathed asking for help, which meant that he always waited until the

situation was a total disaster before he called Jock in. A
prolapse…

It must have been a hell of a delivery to make that
happen so why hadn't Sam called Jock out hours ago?
He hadn't, though, so there was nothing Jock could do
about it now. It was too late to do anything but sigh and
go and tell Tina that he had to leave. Maybe Lloyd and
Sally could run Tina home when the dance ended?
Maybe her pharmacist would. Tina elected neither.

She stood within the proprietary hold of the pharmacist and looked at Jock in concern. 'Oh, Jock, that's too
bad.' Her eyes creased in understanding. Like all doctors, Tina knew what it was like to be interrupted at
every conceivable wrong moment. Then she smiled
apologetically up at Kevin the pharmacist.

'Kevin, if you'll excuse me, I'll go with Jock,' she
said softly, and Jock had to pinch himself to believe he
was hearing correctly. 'He might need an anaesthetist.'

'But—'

'No.'

Kevin and Jock spoke in tandem. Kevin's hold tightened.

'You're not a doctor tonight, Tina,' Kevin growled.
'Unless you're on call… Mark's the full-time anaesthetist. Jock can call on him.'

But Tina looked over to where Mark Spencer was
dancing cheek to cheek with his wife, and shook her
head. Her fiery hair swung free, doing strange things to
the way Jock's knees operated.

'Nope.' She disengaged herself from Kevin's hold and
tucked her arm into Jock's. 'If my date's going to play
doctors then so will I. I only have him for two dates,
you see. I'd best make the most of it. Goodnight, Kevin.
Let's go, Jock.' And she led him out of the hall, with
Jock feeling as if he could be pushed over by a feather.

*   *   *

'You didn't have to come.'

They were almost at the hospital before Jock found the strength to speak, and even then his voice sounded odd. Tina threw him a very odd glance.

'Yes, I did,' she said frankly. 'Kevin's got body odour and his hands sweat. Also he's got only one thing on his mind, and I'm not interested.'

That produced a grin.

'You don't want me to run you home, then?' Jock asked, hoping like hell she'd say no. 'Or call you a cab?'

'Nope. I'm coming with you.' Tina smiled. 'You asked me out, Jock, so you're stuck with me for the evening, like it or not.'

There was the beginnings of a disaster in the labour ward.

Heather Wardrop was a middle aged mother of six children. She'd expected a complication-free delivery, like the other five, but, weakened by multiple births, the uterus had simply inverted. Now Heather was appalled and distressed by the mess she was in, she was in the beginnings of shock, her husband was frantic and Sam Hopper was bleating like a helpless nanny goat.

'Hell, Jock,' he said as Jock walked through the door, and his voice was defensive. 'How was I supposed to guess this might happen? It all just happened so fast. I've never had one do this. God, it looks awful...'

'It looks bad but it's not awful,' Jock said firmly, making a fast visual examination and seeing the fear escalate by the second in Heather and her husband. First step here was to get the shock under control. 'Can you set up an IV line, please, Tina?' Heavens, Sam might at least have done that. 'This isn't all that uncommon as a complication of delivery, and it's easy to fix.' He moved to Heather's side and took her hand, then ignored the bleating doctor behind him to concentrate solely on allaying her terror.

'Hey, there's no problem here, Heather,' he said softly. 'There's no need to look like that. Your body's just a bit too efficient. It's getting so good at pushing out babies that it's pushing out everything else as well. But it's OK. You know when you take off a sock and sometimes it turns inside out. All you need to do is turn it right way around again. That's my job now. Turn you the right way out again.'

'But—'

'Where's the end product here?' Jock asked, his eyes gently smiling and sending out reassurance in waves. From Jock's face you'd think there was no problem at all, and Tina felt a sense of relief start to creep back into the room. The terror ebbed. 'Where's the cause of all the trouble?' He looked around for a crib. 'All this fuss and no baby?'

'Sister…Sister took her to the nursery,' Heather faltered.

'So it's a little girl?'

'Yes.'

'And what are you and Michael going to call her?' Jock was acting like there was all the time in the world. His eyes sent an urgent message to Tina to get the fluids going fast, but his actions were steady and unhurried.

He moved to the sink and scrubbed, ready to do a full examination, then came back, still waiting for an answer. The urgency faded even further, and Heather's terror-filled eyes softened. 'What are you going to call her?' he asked again, and finally the woman focussed on her baby rather than on her fear.

'Marguerite. We'll call her Marguerite,' she whispered. 'After Michael's mother…'

'That's a lovely name. I'll make myself known to

Marguerite very soon,' Jock promised, 'but first we'd better turn this sock back to rights.'

'How...? How...?' It was Michael Wardrop, his face as white as death as he watched what was happening to his wife.

'It's a simple procedure,' Jock told him, 'but it's easier—pain free, in fact—if Heather's asleep while we do it. So if it's OK with you, Heather, Dr Rafter here will give you a quick anaesthetic and then I'll do my sock turning. I'll pop a couple of stitches in to hold you in place while your body heals, and then Bob's your uncle. You'll be fine again.' He smiled. 'OK, Heather?'

'OK.' The woman was sagging with relief, terror giving way to absolute exhaustion. She'd had enough. Fear was fading and exhaustion was taking over.

'I guess I do need to ask, though,' Jock said thoughtfully as he examined the damage and suppressed a wince. 'Is it in your plans to have any more babies? I can do a better stitching job here if I know there's no more coming out the way this one did.'

'Oh, Doc, there'll be no more babies,' Heather breathed wearily. 'We wanted this one, but six...well, six is a nice even number and I'm forty-three and Michael's forty-seven. I reckon we'll call it a day. Don't you, Mike?'

'Too right we will,' her husband agreed fervently. 'We hadn't really planned this one. She just sort of slipped through. But now...' He gripped his wife's hand and stared at Jock, with hope building in his eyes. Who knew what Sam's terror had done to these people? Tina thought. In the face of his fear they must have thought Heather was dying. 'You just fix my Heather up, Doc,' he pleaded. 'Please?'

'You don't think we should send her to Sydney?' Sam said nervously from behind them. 'Hell, Jock, this looks...it looks ghastly...'

'It looks a lot worse than it is,' Jock snapped, and his voice was cutting. Sam would have them all in hysterics if he wasn't stopped. Jock turned his back on the man and smiled at Michael and his wife.

'Now, I know Dr Rafter and I look a pretty unlikely pair of doctors,' he told them, 'but underneath the party clothes and Dr Rafter's silk stockings we're extremely competent. Tina's a fine anaesthetist and I've dealt with more prolapses than I'd care to mention. We can fix this if you'll let us. I can send you to Sydney, Heather, but it'll be a long and uncomfortable journey, and there's no need. Do you trust us?' He faced Michael head-on. 'Do you trust us, Mr Wardrop?'

'Gee, I dunno.' For the first time Tina saw the flicker of a smile enter Mike Wardrop's anxiety-ridden eyes. Jock's solid confidence was having its effect. He looked from Tina in her crazy, skimpy dress to Jock in his dinner suit, and then Michael managed to smile down at his wife. 'Do we trust you to these two gladflies, Heather, love? They look like something off the cover of *Vogue*.'

'Oh, yes,' Heather breathed, and she managed a smile herself. Her head sank back wearily on the pillows and she closed her eyes. 'I've always had a thing for men in dinner suits. Sexy as anything, they are. You just leave me be, Michael Wardrop, and let Dr Blaxton do whatever he likes with me. He's more than welcome. Just as long as no one expects me to help!'

She started drifting toward sleep before Tina could even begin to think about an anaesthetic.

It wasn't quite as simple a procedure as Jock had implied. It took two hours in Theatre before they were sure all the damage had been rectified, and Jock was really glad the Wardrops had said it was the end of babies for Heather.

'Because with this amount of stitching the next one's a Caesarean or not at all,' he said grimly, as he stood back from the table. 'Maybe this one should have been a Caesarean anyway. With such a big baby, Sam should have sought specialist advice. If not mine, then someone else's.'

Jock's anger was almost palpable. Tina had been aware of it, barely suppressed, from the time Dr Sam Hopper had yawned as they'd wheeled Heather into Theatre and announced his intention of heading back to bed and leaving Tina and Jock to cope.

'He's just not interested,' Jock had said through gritted teeth. 'Sam closed his books after medical school and he makes no pretence of keeping up with modern knowledge.'

That was all he'd said, whispered through gritted teeth while the nurses were occupied with Heather, but now...with Heather wheeled back to the ward and Jock and Tina alone at the sink, Jock made no effort to control the blast of fury.

'The man's incompetent. Incompetent to try and deliver babies. Doesn't he know the damage he can do? Doesn't he realise the consequences?' Jock's voice was laced with fury, laced with exhaustion and laced with pain.

Jock took Heather's danger seriously, Tina thought. Deadly seriously.

'Jock, Heather's OK now,' she said gently. 'Thanks to you...'

'But what if she'd had a ruptured uterus? Or... So many things to go wrong... Doesn't he know the risk with multigravidas is more than the risk with first-time mothers? According to Sam's notes, Heather's had five big babies... Every single baby over nine pounds, and two of them over ten pounds. This one's ten and a half pounds—Sam must have known it was huge at prenatal checks—and he sails in at the last minute with not the least fear of complications.

'And you know what would have happened if she'd died?' Jock's face was white and drawn as he continued. 'Sam would have shrugged and said "these things happen". They don't *just happen*. Not now. Not with the precautions that should be taken. But I can't be in every place at once to make sure they are, and if doctors won't refer...'

'Is that what you want to do?' Tina asked gently, watching his face. 'Be everywhere at once?'

That stopped him. Jock lifted his face to Tina's, and stared. Then he shook his head, shaking off a nightmare, and, at last, he managed a smile.

'Hell, that makes me sound like a conceited...'

'Like the great obstetrician that you are.' Tina grinned and hoisted herself up to sit on the bench beside the sink. She was wearing a theatre gown over her skimpy red dress and was feeling almost demure. Only her stock-inged legs swung free, hinting at the sexiness of her outfit underneath. 'Hey, Jock...'

'What?' The strain was still in his voice. He looked up, but Tina knew he was hardly seeing her. He was seeing catastrophe—six children without a mother, Michael Wardrop without a wife. He was seeing his own mother. Tina's heart lurched. Jock's heart was on his face. There was anguish in his eyes. Who'd have guessed it? she thought. Who'd have guessed...? The great Jock Blaxton... With a heart big enough to take on the whole world. Dear heaven, she was starting to love him.

Love? The word flashed through her mind like light-ning, flashing to illuminate the sky. That one simple thought showed things which had always been there but had been hidden in the dark until now. It showed her that she was falling in love with a man who had no intention in the world of committing himself to anyone, much less her.

'Hey, Jock...' Unconsciously, Tina's hand reached out to stroke Jock's hair. Her fingers slid through the tangle of deep black curls in an age-old gesture of comfort. A woman, giving comfort to her man.

'There's a new little person in the world because of what's happened here tonight,' she said softly. 'A tiny little girl called Marguerite Wardrop, who has a mother who's going to be fine, thanks to you, Jock.'

Her fingers kept right on stroking, trying desperately to ease his pain. 'You might not be able to save the world, Jock. You might not be able to be everywhere. But you've done your bit for the Wardrop family tonight. You've done your bit for my sister as well, and I think you're wonderful. So, what else do you expect of yourself?'

No answer. Jock was stiff and silent under her fingers, standing before her, not moving, and still his face was etched with pain. Suddenly Tina couldn't bear it. There were ghosts in this man's past, dreadful ghosts. Ghosts that meant he couldn't live with himself, couldn't go forward.

What sort of parents had laid this awful sense of guilt upon his shoulders? she wondered. To blame a child for a mother's death... To bestow on him a guilt that meant that he had to face this pain alone, for ever. There was nothing to do to ease the pain but...but to comfort him in the only way that seemed to make sense. Tina let her other hand drift up to his hair so both sets of fingers were stroking through those magic curls. Thick and thatched and curling, the feel of his hair sent erotic shards through her whole body. Stroking. Stroking.

Then she pulled him forward so that his head was almost on her breast. Tina lowered her face to his, and tilted his unresisting chin up to hers. And kissed him.

CHAPTER SIX

It WAS supposed to be a kiss of comfort, nothing more. Ha!

Whatever was between Jock and Tina—whatever was between this man and this woman—wasn't comfort, but a full-blown volcanic explosion. The moment Tina's lips met Jock's the whole world changed. Or stopped. What was happening here? This was crazy, Tina thought desperately as she felt passion surge between them. Here she was, feeling content that everything had turned out well, and feeling warm and weary and sorry for this big man with his damned handsome face and his lovely thatch of hair and his caring eyes and his ghosts...

But that was all! she told herself. She'd felt sorry for him. Sorry! Sorry wasn't the emotion that slammed into her now. It was naked, fathomless lust. Tina's lips descended onto Jock's and he hadn't wanted to be kissed— she was almost sure of that. It was just that he was numb and exhausted and in no condition to argue—and all of a sudden this lightning bolt hit him and it hit her at the same time and it fused them together like glue.

Heat! The heat was overpowering. Tina was melting inside. There was fire, starting in her lips and working its way downward—sweeping its way downward—burning straight down to her toes and back up again. Sweeping back and forth, washing wave after wave of fire from her toes to the tips of her ears and back down again. And her thighs... Her thighs were screaming a need she'd never known she'd had.

Jock's hands were moving. They rose, almost of their own volition, and they were now holding her waist, bringing her body closer, moving her thighs against him. Tina was somehow sliding off the bench, sliding down to be held against his body, her lips never moving except to open—to deepen the kiss—to demand that Jock's mouth took hers. Her tongue came out all of it own accord. Searching his mouth. Demanding an entry into his moist, wonderful recesses.

Jock. Jock! Her toes were curling upward at the thought of him, at the feel of him! Tina's whole body was curling. Like a burning match, she was flaming beside him—being consumed—taking him to her and offering the heat of her body in return. Jock... Dear God, Jock...

What was happening to her? She knew. She knew! Without doubt, she knew. This feeling had never happened to Tina in her life before, but it was unmistakable. This was her man, this was where she wanted to be.

Jock...

But he didn't want her, he didn't want anyone. Somehow... Somehow Jock pushed her back, an inch...two inches...with Tina whimpering a protest. But she didn't follow. Somehow Tina managed to grip onto that much pride. She let herself be pushed away—held at arm's length and watched by those dark eyes.

Jock watched her with eyes that were almost accusing, but Tina's eyes didn't leave his for a second. She stared straight back and her look didn't falter. She wasn't ashamed that she'd kissed this man. How could she be ashamed? Something was happening to her here that she didn't understand—that she had no hope of understanding because it was so new to her—and she was starting to wonder where it would take her.

This might be a path she'd never travelled before, but Tina knew for certain that whatever she was feeling she wanted it to continue. She'd walk down this path with joy.

But... 'No,' Jock said, and his voice was ragged.

'No?' Amazingly, there was laughter in Tina's voice, though her voice wasn't the least bit steady. 'No? You don't want to ravish me on the theatre floor, Jock, darling? Rats! That's what it felt like for a moment there, and it would have been a first, too!'

Jock's eyes flared. His body stiffened and for a moment Tina thought—hoped—that he'd seize her again, and do just that.

But Jock—somehow—was back in control again, and he didn't want women. Not seriously. Not ever.

'Tina... I'll... I'm sorry.'

'Sorry you kissed me?' Tina chuckled and leaned forward to kiss him again lightly on the lips. He didn't respond, didn't move. Simply stared with those blank, fathomless eyes. 'That's not very nice.'

'I'm not meant to be nice. It's just...'

'I know. You're not in the market for a serious relationship.' Tina nodded, forcing her voice to sound light, making a Herculean effort to keep her voice light. 'I know that. And neither am I, of course. Remember... Remember Peter?'

That got to him, reached through the blankness. Some of the anger flooded back and saved him.

'Peter...'

'Yep, Peter.' Tina's eyes dared to smile up at him and his anger grew.

'You mean, you kiss a man like that when you're going steady with another man?'

'Only when it's you.' There, she'd said it now. He could shove that in his pipe and smoke it.

Jock's eyes narrowed, and blazed with a mixture of anger and passion. 'What the hell's that supposed to mean?'

'Just what I said,' Tina retorted. 'Meaning I never have kissed a man like that, and I don't know why I kissed you like that and if you can explain it then you're welcome to try. I'm all ears.'

Silence.

Tina finally managed to find the courage to kiss him again, lightly, but not with passion.

'Jock, leave it,' she said, and only she knew the effort it cost her to keep her voice light. She was starting to believe she was falling heavily in love with this man, but admitting it... Heavens, admitting it would make him run a mile. 'We're obviously good at creating electricity. So maybe we could interest the State Energy Board. Or maybe...' She sighed at the look in his eyes. 'Maybe we could just check that Marguerite Wardrop's OK and then maybe we could go to bed.'

'Bed...' Jock's tone was blank.

'I mean our own separate beds,' Tina said, and there was a tiny spurt of anger in her own voice then. How dared he! she thought suddenly. The man was behaving like a moralistic prig and now he was making her feel like a tramp. 'What else would I mean? What else when I'm happily settled with my Peter?'

Only, of course, she wasn't.

There was no talk of another date. Tina was left under no illusions that Jock wanted anything further to do with her. But she couldn't let it rest there. She couldn't. Tina spent the next week, trying to figure out just what she was feeling. Trying to avoid Jock Blaxton and failing. He had a night delivery of twins and a woman with a miscarriage while she was on duty, and both times they had to work together. Jock was stiff and formal and distant—but by the end of the week Tina figured she was going quietly nuts.

Dear God, she was in love. She was totally, absolutely and irrevocably in love—with someone who wanted nothing more to do with her. But it wasn't in Tina's nature to go quietly nuts. If she was going nuts, then

she'd do it in style, and do it honourably. There was no
way she could continue to go out with Peter—not now.
Not now she knew what it was to be kissed by a man
like Jock.

Sure, there was a strong possibility that Jock would
never kiss her again in his life. He'd certainly try not to.
But she *knew* now. She knew what it felt like, and
Peter's kisses were going to be a pale comparison. Peter
telephoned her on the night after the dance and she tried
to be interested in the news from Sydney. She tried.
Then Peter tried to be interested in what was happening
in Gundowring and that didn't work either.

So Tina took a deep breath and said since they'd be
spending so much time apart maybe they should feel free
to date other people—and was only faintly piqued by
the trace of relief in Peter's voice as he agreed. Yeah,
OK. She and Peter really didn't suit long term, but it
had been a comfortable relationship for two busy people.
So where did that leave her now?

It left her here. It left her in Gundowring with Christie
and the children. They were all that mattered.

At least things were good on that front. But Christie
thought Jock was wonderful and that was a bit hard to
take when she was trying hard to tell herself that Jock
wasn't so fantastic.

Christie went to see Jock on the Monday of her appointment and came back bubbling. For the first time
since Rose's birth she was smiling, without Tina working on it.

'Oh, Tina, Dr Blaxton's just lovely,' she told her sister. 'He's made me see things in such a new light. He's
found out who Ray's with now.' Christie shook her head
in astonishment. 'And he made me laugh about it!'

'Laugh?'

'I couldn't believe it myself,' Christie admitted.
'But...well, Ray's forty-seven and Skye...the girl Ray's

with…is seventeen. He painted such a picture of what Ray must be going through! Dr Blaxton's idea of purgatory would be taking a teenager to discos when he's forty-seven. He says Ray's chosen his own punishment and I should count my blessings.'

'I did try telling you that,' Tina said cautiously, and Christie's smile widened. She gave her sister a hug.

'I know. I know you did, Tina, love, but maybe I wasn't ready to hear it. Or maybe I needed an outsider to lay it on the line. And Dr Blaxton has such a way with him…' Her smile turned to a downright grin, mischief included. The old Christie was flooding back.

'And I'll tell you what else. Dr Blaxton rang the Department of Social Security and they say they can garnishee Ray's wages. That means support for our children comes out of Ray's wages and is sent to me before he even sees what he's earned. And that happens no matter where in Australia Ray goes.'

'Is that right?'

'He says it is. Oh, Tina, Ray left because he hated paying for the kids… But now… As well as supporting Ally and Tim and Rose, he'll be paying the expenses of his seventeen-year-old lover.' Christie's smile faded. 'I don't think that'll be all that much fun—do you?'

'You don't feel sorry for him, do you?' Tina asked incredulously, and Christie nodded.

'I do. Tina, for the first time I do—and that's a healing in itself. For the first time I feel not just anger and hurt but disgust with Ray that he could do this. And sorry for what he's lost.' Christie's lovely smile flashed back. 'But that's not stopping me applying for garnishment.'

'Oh, Christie…'

'I think he's the best doctor,' Christie said happily. 'When are you going out with him again?'

'He hasn't asked me,' Tina confessed, and Christie stared.

'So when has that ever stopped you with a man?' she demanded. 'Ask *him*, then. For heaven's sake, Tina. If I wasn't sworn off men for life—or at least until my stretch marks fade—I'd ask him out myself. Tina, Jock is seriously wonderful. Go for it.'

'He isn't serious.'

'So he's just plain wonderful. You get serious for both of you. Ask him!'

Ask him… Easier said than done.

Tina spent a few days working on her courage and telling herself she was a dope for even attempting such a thing. But every time she talked herself out of it she'd turn a corner in the hospital corridor and there Jock would be, stethoscope dangling across his white coat, his dark eyes twinkling at some joke a nurse was making…. The man was seriously wonderful…

Christie was dead right, Tina decided. Jock was the most desirable man she'd ever met in her life, and she wasn't going to get one inch further with the man unless she did the running.

So ask! Ask, Tina Rafter. Ask! So she did. Tina waited until she had him alone—no mean feat itself in a busy hospital—in the nursery. He was checking his charges—four lusty babies—and Tina watched him through the windows, moving from crib to crib, before she entered.

He did love babies! The look on his face as he lifted young Marguerite Wardrop up into his arms… There was no real need for him to lift her but as Jock looked down at her, unaware of anyone watching, Tina could see for herself what was written in his soul. It was nonsense that this man didn't want a family, she thought. Sure, he was afraid. But his desire was written in his eyes. He wanted one of these babies for his own. There wasn't one too many babies in the world for Jock. There were too few!

He'd make the best father, Tina thought as she watched his gentle hands—and his smile which had her heart doing back flips. He'd make the best lover! Tina's thighs started heating up all by themselves.

Ask him!

She took a deep breath and swung open the nursery door. Before her thighs started flaming right here in the hospital corridor!

'Hi.'

Jock looked up from Marguerite and his smile faded.

'Hi.' He placed the baby back gently in the cot, adjusted her covers and then looked at his watch. By which time he had his face nicely under control. Stiff and formal. 'What are you still doing in the hospital?' he asked.

As a welcome it was about as warm as a bucket of cold water.

'I work here.' Tina managed a smile. 'You employed me again. Remember?'

Remember? How could he not remember? Jock's face closed even more. 'I meant you're due to go off duty at seven a.m.' He scowled at his watch, as if it had betrayed him. 'That's an hour ago.'

'I know,' Tina told him. 'I waited. I wanted to see you.'

If it was possible for his face to close any more it did then. It shut down all over the place. As far as his face was concerned, Jock was out for lunch!

'Why?'

'Gee, you sound friendly.'

'I'm busy.'

'Yeah, I can see that.' Tina grinned. 'So busy you have time to cuddle each of these babies in turn. Frantic schedule, Dr Blaxton.'

'What did you want to talk to me about?'

'Our second date.'

That reached him. Tina saw an expression flit behind

his eyes that she wasn't the least sure she understood. Like a lion suddenly unsure that the prey he was about to kill didn't have tusks. Sharp tusks that could kill.

'Hey, it's only a wedding,' she said hurriedly. 'I need a partner, and I can't take Peter.'

'Why can't you take Peter?'

'We've split up,' Tina said mournfully. 'Isn't that sad? We've been going out for nearly a year, and now we find we're not suited.'

'Why aren't you suited?' The wariness was there in force. Tina felt she was practically *wearing* tusks. So what answer would take the wariness away?

'Peter wants a wife and babies and I don't want to be a wife and mother,' she said. It was true. Not with Peter, she didn't. 'I want to have some fun, Jock, while I'm still young enough to enjoy it.'

'Yeah?'

'Yeah.' Tina leaned over young Cameron Croxton and stopped looking at Jock, taking the heat right off him. When in doubt refer to work.

'Hey, Cameron's jaundice looks almost better,' she said. 'He just looks tanned now, instead of like he's been eating too much saffron. That's great.'

'His bilirubin levels are way down and still dropping.'

'He'll be able to go home, then?'

'Yes—except his dad wants him to be circumcised. I can't talk him out of it.'

'Straight away?'

'He says his son's not complete until it's done,' Jock said morosely. 'I guess I'll have to do it or they'll get some backyarder to operate, but I hate it. Especially when he's been so ill. We're only just on top of the jaundice.'

Tina nodded in sympathy. Once little boys had been circumcised as a matter of course in the days immediately after their birth, no matter what condition they'd been in. The old belief had been that it didn't hurt new-borns—but it did. It hurt them very much and in some it induced shock. Occasionally—rarely, but often enough for most doctors to have seen a tragic example—it caused infection and death.

So, if it had to be done, it was best to be done by a competent doctor, using local anaesthetic. Most doctors now asked that it be done when the babies weren't so new, but if Cameron's parents insisted then there was little for Jock to do but perform the operation. As he said, if it meant that much to them, if Jock didn't do it someone else would.

Tina lifted young Cameron from his cot and gave him a hug. 'It's a hard world out there,' she told the fuzzy little head, and hugged him again. 'But Dr Blaxton's good. The best. He'll look after you.' She looked over to Jock and his wary look was back again.

'About this wedding...' she said.

'Tina...'

'Jock, are you afraid to go out with me?' she demanded, and Jock's eyes widened.

'Well?'

Despite his wariness, Jock found himself smiling. 'Tina, in the circles I was brought up in it was impolite for young ladies to ask men out—and if the man refused it was even more impolite for her to call him a coward.'

'It's just lucky I'm not a young lady, then.' Tina's eyes locked on his, challenging. 'This wedding is this Saturday at four o'clock. You're not on call. I checked. The church and reception are both close enough for you to leave if there's a baby needs delivering. I'm brides-maid so you'll get to mingle with the other guests while I do my duties. I only need a token partner to sit in the partner spot while I eat my dinner. A token partner, Jock Blaxton. That's all. And who knows? You might even end up having fun.'

He might. Maybe. But maybe that was just what Jock was afraid of.

Jock didn't have fun, but it was no fault of the wedding. The tension between himself and Tina was almost palpable.

The wedding itself was great—a huge affair to which the whole district was invited. Harry was a local farmer. Mary was the local school teacher. Harry played football and cricket and darts and Mary played netball and tennis and hockey, and every sports club was there in force. As well as that, both families were huge and even the district dogs were showing a fair representation.

The church was out on the headland and the little chapel was overflowing. The reception was in a nearby shearing shed, and the bush band was quite simply the best Jock had ever heard. But, as Tina had promised, he really was only her token partner. He got to sit beside Tina at the formal part of the dinner but afterwards the tables were hauled back and Tina, as chief bridesmaid, was whirled around and around the shed in the arms of one man after another. It was almost as if she was avoiding him.

She was.

Tina was dressed much more demurely today than at the hospital dance in her simple white bridesmaid's dress that fell in soft folds to her ankles, covering her nicely from the neck down. Demure, but still wonderful. She was tense, though.

It had been a mistake, Tina thought sadly, inviting Jock. The man looked at her with the eyes of a man stepping into a river full of piranhas. Jock might have agreed to accompanying her, but he hadn't agreed to anything else.

Damn the man! Somehow she had to let him see she wasn't about to launch herself at him. She wouldn't cling like a limpet and threaten his damned solitude. He made no move to stay with her as the evening progressed and, short of making herself seem a lovesick fool, Tina had no choice but to let him be. Drat the man!

He had to dance with her once. After the bridal waltz there was a dance where people were expected to stay with their partners so Jock couldn't escape. Tina danced well but Jock held her rigidly in his arms and she knew that, given the choice, he'd be home like a shot.

Tina had her pride. Two circles of the dance floor and she was getting angry. It helped. And then she found something to distract her, which helped even more. A group of teenagers was drinking heavily outside the shed, and Tina was suddenly more concerned with them than she was with Jock.

'They're only just eighteen,' she told Jock. She'd allowed herself to be deliberately diverted by the teenagers, but now she was truly troubled. 'I wish their parents would intervene. They're drinking far too much for their own good.'

This was a new sensation for Jock. Sure, he hadn't wanted this dance, but now... To have a woman in his arms and not have her full attention... He'd meant to stay aloof, apart. The fact that it was Tina calling the shots now made him want to haul her in close and make her pay attention. Or maybe that's what he wanted to do anyway.

But Tina was still watching the teenagers. He followed her gaze, and some of the tension he was feeling found a vent in anger. The teenagers were drinking like idiots, mixing spirits with beer and generally becoming louder and more aggressive by the minute.

'Their parents are here,' Tina said. 'Why don't they stop them? I wonder if I should do anything.'

'What could you do?'

'I don't know. Say something...'

'It's not our business,' Jock said brusquely. God, she was lovely. 'And they won't be stupid enough to drive.' His eyes rested on the teenagers for a long moment. 'Stupid fools. If they were my kids…'

'They won't be, though, will they, Jock?' Tina said, and her voice was infinitely sad. Infinitely weary. The hands holding her were still rigid and formal. Giving nothing. 'Not ever. Responsibility isn't your scene.' She bit her lip—and suddenly pushed herself away. 'No. I'm sorry, Jock. Maybe…maybe tonight was a mistake.'

Heavens, if he held her like this one moment longer she'd burst into tears. 'I…I need to dance with somebody else.'

That was it! End of dance, end of allocated time with Tina. But Jock found his eyes following her around the shed as he whirled his own succession of partners across the worn shearing-shed boards. Hell! This was driving him nuts. This was *it*, he told himself. The end. The last time he'd spend any time with her at all except at work. She couldn't possibly ask him out after this—not if he was distant enough—and he wouldn't ask her. He wouldn't—because it was too damned dangerous.

He could start thinking about that London job again. Set things in motion so he could leave as soon as Gina and Struan came back. London seemed a long way away. And then the Pride of Erin had him changing partners yet again and Tina was suddenly beside him again, laughing in his arms. Soft. Delicious. Desirable.

'Having fun?' Her lovely eyes teased him, as though there was nothing between them at all, and Jock couldn't begin to guess the effort it cost her.

'Mmm.' That was one stupid lie. 'You?'

'I love weddings.' She did so it wasn't a lie.

'Yet you won't marry your Peter?'

'No.' She twirled out from him as he spun her around, and then pulled back into his side. She seemed to fit, as if there were a niche specially built in his ribs to accommodate her.

'You really don't want to get married?' he demanded, unbelieving, and she shook her wonderful hair.

'I really don't. At least—that's my story and I'm sticking to it.'

'Why?'

'Because every time I look twice at you, you get twitchy—like you're being pursued by a killer shark,' she snapped, her smile fading. 'So let's not get paranoid, Dr Blaxton. Just relax and have fun.' She managed to smile up at him and then took two steps forward to her new partner—and was whisked on in the dance circle, and Jock was left with all the wind knocked right out of him.

Tina avoided him completely after that for the rest of the night. Or he avoided her. Or maybe both. But they had to drive home together. Tina had come in the bridal car so she had no other way of getting home. They left at two in the morning, and both were so tense as they left that Tina was close to screaming.

The few stayers were still dancing but Mary and her Harry had left, tin cans and horseshoes trailing in a clattering stream from the back of Harry's farm truck. The oldies had long since packed up and gone home. Tina took a deep breath and tucked her arm possessively into Jock's arm. Reclaiming her man?

'OK, Prince Charming. Cinderella's about to turn into a pumpkin. Bring on your glass coach.'

'Isn't that a glass slipper?'

'Whatever. But I'm done with slippers.' She yawned, kicked off her bridesmaid shoes and walked barefoot with him over the paddocks to the car, trying to act casual.

They weren't the only ones leaving. In the distance some teenagers were fighting about car keys. They could hear them in the distance as they approached. It was the same teenagers they'd watched drinking.

'Hell, Andrew, you're not fit to drive. Leave the car here. We'll get a ride.'

'I'm fine. I've only had a couple of beers.'

'A couple! A couple of dozen more like. Plus the whisky.'

'Look, there's damn-all taxis out here. Shut up and get in!'

Tina and Jock heard their voices, carrying clearly across the paddocks, and looked at each other in alarm in the moonlight.

'Hi,' Jock yelled, and started forward, but it was too late. They were still too far away. The teenagers had piled into the car and the ancient vehicle lurched erratically towards the gate.

'Hell,' Jock said, and reached into his pocket for his mobile phone.

'What are you doing?' Tina stared after the car in consternation. She didn't need to be told that this was a disaster waiting to happen.

'I'm calling the police,' Jock said bluntly as the teenagers' car squealed onto the highway on two wheels. 'If that mob of young idiots aren't stopped, they'll kill themselves—if not someone else. Where the hell are their parents?'

It created even more tension, but there was nothing they could do about the teenagers. They were driving at such speed there was no way Jock or Tina could catch them. Tina settled into the passenger seat of Jock's lovely little car and was silent.

So was Jock.

Nothing had happened between them, Tina thought sadly. Nothing! Maybe she should have clung to him tonight. But... She knew that clinging would make this man run a mile. So...nothing had happened. Jock was telling himself the same thing. He'd been worried that he'd make a fool of himself tonight. Take things too far. Give Tina the wrong idea...

But nothing had happened. That was what Jock wanted, he told himself savagely. So leave it that way. Just get this girl home, leave her there and get on with his life. It was what he wanted—wasn't it? He stared ahead bleakly at the ribbon of highway—and then the night erupted in a ball of fire before them and the thought of what he wanted from his life suddenly had no relevance at all.

CHAPTER SEVEN

JOCK'S foot hit the brake as a boom with the force of a vast bomb smashed across the soft music of Jock's car stereo, and fire lit the sky. All Tina and Jock could see was flames. The fire was so huge it was practically towering above them.

Dear God. Without speaking, Jock put his foot to the accelerator again and his little car crept forward. Fearful of what they would find at the source of the flame, they drove forward three hundred yards, slowly around the next corner, and then there was a hill, rising to a crest... There was no way they were driving up that crest. Beyond was the fire. There were flames, leaping a hundred feet into the sky, on the other side. Without exchanging one word—there was just nothing to say to each other, nothing in the face of such fear—Tina and Jock left the car and ran up the hill to reach the unspeakable horror on the other side.

Before they reached the crest Jock had collected himself enough for priorities. He fell one step behind Tina as he fumbled in his inner pocket for his phone. Tina could hardly hear him for the roaring of the flames.

'Kate... Doc Blaxton here. I'm on Slatey Creek Road near Black Hill. There's been a major crash. I need ambulance and fire engine...fire engines. There's a major fire. Police, too, Kate. Send everything you've got. No. There have to be casualties but I don't know how many. Assume the worst. Fast, Kate. Now!'

Jock clicked closed the mouthpiece and reached the top of the crest two seconds after Tina, and stood beside her for one long moment, appalled. What they saw took their breath away. There was a petrol tanker…vast and burning out of control. It must have veered off the highway, before exploding, because it was thirty yards from the road on their right. It was now a massive, roaring ball of flames, consuming the night.

There was a car below the crest, on their left. It was lit by the flames but it wasn't alight. The car had a crumpled, mangled rear but it was still whole. Still safe. It was on the other side of the highway to the burning truck, and the same group of teenagers Tina and Jock had seen not five minutes before were struggling from the car, dazed and shaken.

Tina swung around to face the truck again—and stared. Dear God, that couldn't be the driver! Could it? There was a man, staggering across the paddock toward the road. His body was a black shadow lit by the inferno behind. A man… A man alive from that awfulness.

Jock had already seen him and was running, striding out with a speed Tina could never match, down towards that blackened figure. Tina was left to follow. Miraculously the man appeared to be almost unhurt. He was singed around the edges. He was bleeding from a gash on the face but he was still on his feet, and the fact that his shirt was still intact on his back meant that the singeing was only minor.

Tina practically sobbed in relief as she reached him. Jock was supporting the man, helping him away from the fireball. The heat was unbearable. Tina shoved herself under the man's other shoulder and together she and Jock half dragged, half carried him back toward the road.

'Is there anyone else in the truck?' Jock was asking urgently across the roar of the flames. The heat was catching in his throat, making speech almost impossible, but the question had to be asked. 'Anyone?'

The man shook his head, unable to make his mouth frame the word 'no'. His legs were sagging under him.

Released, he would have crumpled where he stood. Who knew what massive effort he must have made to get clear of the burning wreck? Another boom echoed across the paddocks and the blast of heat was like a physical blow, knocking them forward.

Tina lurched and regained her balance, the heat searing through the thin fabric of her bridesmaid's dress. This was not *de rigueur* fireman's clothing, she thought grimly, but it was all she had. She had no choice but to stay and help. The heat was growing more intense by the minute. Jock didn't falter and neither did Tina. Finally they had the man on the other side of the road near the teenagers' car where the fire was just a vast menacing presence, close enough to heat way past comfort but not close enough to damage.

They lowered the driver onto the grass verge and Jock knelt to give him a decent examination. Tina stayed standing and looked around her, taking her time now, missing nothing. She was performing triage, assessing priorities. Tina's training slipped back into force and, crazy bridesmaid's dress and satin sandals or not, she was now every inch a doctor.

Jock could manage here. The driver was so shocked he couldn't speak. The gash on his face was bleeding profusely but Jock was already ripping off his jacket to form a pressure pad. The man was shaking like a leaf and sobbing, but there seemed no sign of anything more life-threatening than the gash and some burns. So check the teenagers.

How many were there? One. Two. Three. Four. There were four kids huddled around the car in various stages of distress. Tina thought back to the group she'd seen by the car back at the shearing shed and she did a mental head count of her memory. Four. Yes. Four.

Good grief. Relief hit her with almost physical force. Did this mean they were going to get out of this night

without major casualties? If the driver of the truck was
OK and these four were accounted for...

But then... Tina looked closely at their car and felt a
surge of fear as she looked. This didn't make sense.
There must be... No. Maybe she was wrong. Dear God,
she'd never hoped so much to be wrong in her entire
life.

'Are you OK?' she asked the first teenager as she
reached his side. His girlfriend was vomiting in the
dust—a mixture of drunkenness and shock, Tina
thought—and let her be. 'Are any of you hurt?'

'Doc...'

The boy recognised her. Tina looked closely at the
boy's face in the firelight and recognised a lad she'd
treated for a football injury a week before. 'Oh, Doc...'

'Simon, is anyone hurt?' she asked sharply, and
gripped his shoulders, forcing him to focus through the
shock.

'Andrew thinks he's broken his arm, and Syl...Syl's
hurt her chest and she's sick. But the car... There's people...in the car...'

'Is there someone else in the car?' Tina demanded,
trying to block out the fearful thought that had slammed
into her head a moment before. She took two steps towards it before Simon stopped her.

'Doc, no. Not...not our car. The...the car that hit the
tanker.'

There are moments in life best forgotten. This was
one of them.

Tina turned slowly and stared at the tanker, and then
she stared some more, willing Simon to be imagining
things. Willing him to be wrong. There was no other car
that Tina could see. There was no other crash site than
this car here and the burning tanker. Nothing. She turned
slowly around, her eyes searching the fire-lit scene.

Nothing from this angle! Just a tanker, alone and burning. But... But...

Another look at Simon and she knew the boy wasn't imagining it. Simon's face was a blank reflection of her own terror, and the teenagers' car wasn't badly enough damaged to explain this carnage. To explain why the truck was smashed and burning on the other side of the highway. Dear God...

There must be another car, then, she thought, and her stomach gave a sickening lurch of horror. But where was it? She knew. There was only one answer. And then she was running back to the grass on the other side of the road, lurching crazily in her silly satin sandals as she ran. She couldn't rip them off—not when there were bits of burning debris flying through the night, setting off small sparks of fire in the grass.

Tina ran on regardless. Not straight towards the tanker but behind it. She couldn't go close. The heat was far too intense. She heard Jock yell from somewhere behind her as she ran, but she ignored him and kept on running. If she was right... If she was right, there would be nothing she could do. She knew that.

But she had to know...

Behind and back so she could see the other side of the fire. Running. Holding her hand to her mouth to block the debris from blowing against her, from breathing in ash and petrol vapour. Running so she could see... And it was there. The full horror. The crumpled, mangled mess of a family sedan, wedged in somehow against the side of the tanker as it burned, burning as part of it.

And what she could see... Dear God... Tina sank down onto the grass and closed her eyes. And it took her a long time before she could find the courage to open them.

*   *   *

Jock and Tina worked steadily, numb with shock but working with the sheer force of need. The rest of Gundowring's medical community turned out in force, and it seemed they were all needed.

The driver had second-degree burns to his face and hands. He'd lost some hair and too much blood, but he'd live. Recovering from shock, he'd live.

'He deserves to,' the police chief told Tina as he came into the hospital to get statements from the teenagers. 'You know, he slammed into the car and if he'd stopped—if he'd slammed on his brakes and stopped— then there'd be seven dead instead of three. The kids' car would have burned too.'

'As it was,' the police chief went on grimly, 'by the look of the tyre marks, he realised his load would most likely explode after such an impact so he accelerated again. Got the truck thirty yards off the road and then jumped clear. It wasn't his fault that the other sedan was smashed and caught against the side. His rig was so big it just dragged the car with it.'

'Were they...?' Tina had to ask. 'Were they...?'

The police chief shook his head, knowing without her finishing the question what she'd wanted to know. 'I reckon they were killed instantly,' he said. 'Sure, they were burned but the car was so badly smashed first that they couldn't have been aware... I'd say it was instantaneous.'

'But how did it happen?' Tina shook her head in horror. 'How...?'

'Bloody kids,' the policeman growled. 'It's early days yet—the police accident investigation squad are on their way now—but by the look of it the kids pulled out to overtake the Croxtons on the crest. The Croxtons had been to a family christening party for the baby and were coming home late. They were travelling too damned fast as well. The kids came up over the hill and pulled out to pass them. When the kids saw the tanker they just veered straight back in front of the Croxtons' car. The Croxtons' car will have clipped theirs and been swung sideways in front of the tanker. End of story.'

The big man's voice cracked. 'Bloody kids. Bloody alcohol. We got Doc Blaxton's call from the wedding, warning us the kids were driving drunk, but we couldn't reach them fast enough.'

Tina bit her lip, closed her eyes on the sickening memory—and went back to work. There was nothing else to do. When the world comes crashing down just pick up the pieces and start over... Lloyd and Mark came in and took over with the truck driver. Tina and Sally coped with the teenagers.

They stabilised Sylvia and readied her for transfer by air ambulance to Sydney. She had broken ribs and a punctured lung, and their fear was pneumothorax. Maybe if she hadn't been so drunk they could have operated at Gundowring, but as it was, they'd have to wait for the alcohol to wear off, so they may as well use the time getting her the best surgeon possible.

'And it's not me,' Sally told Tina in a voice that shook. 'Not tonight. I can't operate. Liz Croxton is... Liz Croxton was my friend.'

Sally choked on a sob and Tina thought for the hundredth time how hard it was to be a doctor in a small town. You were too damned involved. And she thought about Jock. As an obstetrician, after the initial first aid there had been little for Jock to do here. Lloyd and Mark and Sally and Tina had their hands full, coping with shock, fractures, burns and drunkenness, but there was a worse job to be done—and Jock had volunteered. Someone had to do it.

Jock had stayed at the scene to supervise the removal of the dead couple from the wreck. The dead couple and their tiny baby, Cameron Croxton, the baby Jock had delivered only two weeks ago.

Tina worked on steadily, but her thoughts were on Jock, lifting what remained of that tiny baby from the burned-out wreck…

She inserted a saline drip into the second girl in the teenagers' car—the girl had been dry-retching non-stop for an hour and the retching showed no sign of abating. Dead drunk, the girl abused her and tore the drip out— and Tina still knew who had the worst job of the night.

The teenagers' parents began to arrive, terrified, appalled and angry in turn. Tina settled them as best she could. Somehow the town had to come to terms with the fact that these young people had caused three deaths. All the teenagers would desperately need the support of their parents in the face of the town's anger. Without it, they could well go under.

So Tina and Sally talked and talked—talked each set of parents through their shock and saw them reunited with their teenagers—and each of them held back the anger burning inside. What were eighteen-year-olds doing, driving dead drunk? These parents must have known the kids had been drinking, and yet they'd left them…

Recriminations were useless. Anger was useless. The dead were dead. Take care of the living.

By five in the morning there was no more to be done. Tina borrowed the hospital car and drove home as weary as she'd ever felt in her life before. She didn't make it home. In the end, she couldn't make herself go. At home Christie would wake if Tina arrived at five a.m. and get up and ask her how her night had gone, and Tina couldn't bear telling her. Not yet. She'd have to tell it calmly, matter-of-factly, so as not to risk Christie plummeting back into that well of depression she was only just climbing from.

And there was Jock…

Tina hadn't seen Jock since she'd gone with the
burned driver in the ambulance. She'd left Jock at the
scene, facing the unfaceable. Jock, the strong one. Just
how strong was he? Unconsciously, Tina turned her
hands on the steering-wheel until her little car was facing
west, facing the beach where Jock had his cottage. She
had a choice here, but there was suddenly no choice.

To distress Christie or to comfort Jock... To comfort
Christie or find comfort in Jock? It was no choice. No
choice at all.

Jock was home, his car in his driveway. For a moment
Tina hesitated, but only for a moment. The lights were
on inside the house so he'd be awake. Tina sat outside
for a long moment and let her thoughts drift over what
Jock had faced tonight.

Jock might be strong, but there was only so much
strength a man could show without breaking. Underneath, he bled. Jock might show the face of a man who
stood alone and was so strong he needed no one—but
Tina knew better. How, she didn't know, but she knew!
Now she couldn't bear that he was alone so Tina parked
the car and went right on in.

There was no answer to her knock on the front door.
Tina gave a tentative push and the door swung wide.

'Jock?'

No answer.

He couldn't have been home for long, she thought,
and he surely couldn't be asleep yet. Not after this night.
Slowly Tina walked from room to room, calling. No one.
She shouldn't be here, she thought bleakly. She was tres-
passing, intruding on his personal space, but she couldn't
bear to go.

'Jock?' She swung open the back door and walked
outside.

He was there. The little house was set on the beachfront, its front door facing the road but its back doors

and windows leading straight down to a sandy cove beneath the headland. The first rays of the dawn were tinging the horizon, and Tina could see Jock's long, lean body pacing the foreshore. Alone.

He must always have been alone, Tina thought suddenly. He'd spent ten years with a dying mother and a father who blamed him for everything, and then the rest of his life accepting that blame. So, of course, Jock had learned to be alone. But he wouldn't be alone now. Not now! Not if she could help it.

Tina slipped off her crazy bridesmaid's sandals—heavens, she was still wearing the stained and ruined chiffon—and ran lightly down across the sand to meet him. Her heart was beating crazily in her chest. He must let her close. He must! She needed him so much.

'Jock?'

'Tina?' Jock stopped and stared up the beach at the approaching figure. 'Tina.'

It wasn't a welcome. The way he said her name was flat, devoid of any emotion at all—drained.

'Oh, Jock.' Without the slightest trace of self-consciousness, Tina went straight up to him, took his hands in hers and held on hard, whether he wanted the contact or not. She desperately needed the link. 'Jock, I had to come.'

'What are you doing here?' Still there was no emotion. Nothing.

'I need you,' she said softly, and closed her eyes and swallowed. She gripped his hands even tighter, but kept her eyes closed and said a thousand silent prayers in her head—all the same prayer.

'Jock, we've finished at the hospital,' she said in a voice that faltered. 'The driver's stabilised. His wife's beside him. Except for Sylvia, the teenagers are all OK. They're with their parents. Sally's gone home with Lloyd. Mark's gone home to Margaret. Meg Preston's come in to take over for the rest of the night and to-morrow she'll go home to her Rob. But... But I couldn't wake up Christie and I needed someone. I needed you.'

Silence.

There was only the sound of the gentle surf, the waves washing back and forth across the sand. In. Out. It surged in time with Tina's breathing. Tina gripped Jock's hands and held hard. She was fighting here for something she hardly understood. Fighting for him to need her as much as she needed him.

'Jock...' She let her head fall forward and touch his chest. He'd worn a dinner suit to the wedding. Heaven knew what sort of state the dinner suit was in now. His coat was gone, used as a pad to stop the driver's bleed-ing, and his shirt was open halfway down his chest, ripped and stained.

'I'm so sorry it had to be you who coped with...who coped with the little one,' she whispered. 'It must have torn you apart.'

'It didn't... I'm OK...' Jock's voice was harsh and cracked. 'Hell, Tina, I don't need—'

'You don't need anyone,' she murmured, and her fin-gers moved within his hands. His hands were rigid, not responding at all to her clasp, but her fingers still stroked, pleaded. 'Jock, don't. Don't try to do this on your own. You deliver a tiny baby two weeks ago and you love him. You can't disguise it from me, Jock, no matter how much you hide it from the world. Somehow you love each and every one of the babies you deliver and you use it to compensate for all the love you should have been given yourself.'

'I don't—'

'It's true,' Tina said harshly, and her eyes flew open to look up at him in the faint dawn light. 'I know. Because I love you, Jock. God knows why. But some-how...I've fallen for you hard and I can read you like a book. So tonight...I know what you'll have gone through when you had to lift Cameron Croxton from that car. It'll have torn you in two. And now... Now you come home alone and you pace the beach and you shove it all inside, like a physical thing that can be swallowed and got rid of and forgotten. Only it can't, Jock, it can't. All the hurt... You have to share. You must.'

Slowly—infinitely gently—she released her hold on his hands. She placed her arms around him and held him close—her slight body moulding itself to his. Whether he willed it or not, she was giving him comfort in the only way she knew. And Tina knew exactly what she was doing, with blinding clarity she knew. She was offering her body in the age-old way of women. Some hurts were just too deep for words.

For some hurts there was only one comfort, there was only one's body. One's home. Jock was her love, her home, and she must be his. Somewhere here the line became blurred and indistinct. Whether Tina was offering comfort or pleading for it herself she didn't know. Who knew? It suddenly didn't matter at all.

'I should have done something,' he said in a voice that cracked. 'Tina, we saw they were drinking...'

'I know. I've been thinking that over and over... But, Jock, there was no way we could have expected them to drive. That was their parents' responsibility.'

'They shouldn't be allowed to have kids if they won't accept that...'

'I know. But that doesn't mean the whole world has to be bleak, Jock. What happened to your mother... What happens to the rest of the world... Jock, don't let it destroy you. Let me close. Please...'

She slipped her hands up under his shirt and ran her fingers along the hard contours of his back. She felt him shudder but she didn't falter.

'Jock, let it go,' she whispered. 'Let it go. Just admit

that you need me. I need you as much as you need me. God knows, I need you more. I love you, Jock. And I can't… Jock, I can't handle tonight…without you.'

And she stood on tiptoe in the sand and she kissed him.

CHAPTER EIGHT

FOR one long moment Tina thought Jock wouldn't respond. For one long moment she thought that he really would stand alone. He'd reject her body and her longing, as he'd learned to reject his own emotional need. But the night had been too long. Too long and too dreadful, and Tina was holding him, kissing him and longing for him to respond—aching for him to respond. He could feel the ache in her lips, and the coldness that was piercing his body right to the bone was warmed by her. The ice was slowly thawing, whether he willed the thaw or not.

He had faced death tonight—he had faced horror—and Tina was offering life. She was offering him a way to go on and he'd have to be superhuman to resist her loveliness and her comfort tonight.

So with a moan that spoke of sheer desperation—of the coming to the end of a cold and lonely road—Jock gathered her yielding body to his and kissed her back.

Not softly. Not that. Jock kissed her fiercely, with a burning, searing need that shook both their bodies with its intensity, and the moment he let his mouth respond to hers both of them knew where this would lead. There was only one possible ending to this night if both of them were to find some measure of sanity.

Somehow they managed to get back to the house, though afterwards Tina was unsure how. She must have been carried, she thought, but if she had been, her mouth never left Jock's, not for an instant. Somehow they made it across the sand, through the back door and into Jock's bedroom, where the big, barren bed lay waiting.

It didn't have long to wait. They were breathless, frantic with passion and frantic with desire. Tina clung to Jock as if she were drowning and he was melting into her. Burning into her. There was no hesitation now. They were one force, united, one body. Jock's mouth devoured her, his hands claiming her, stroking the smooth, soft curves of her breasts, moving down to cup her thighs and lift...

To bring her body close... Closer...

Their clothing was in the way. It was stupidly, frantically, in the way—of no import at all—only there to act as a barrier, and the last thing these two lovers needed was a barrier. Tina heard the chiffon rip as it came away from her body and she didn't care at all. Her hands were frantically doing the same undressing of Jock and she'd rip too if she must. She was searching... wanting...fighting to get her body next to his.

They must both have been a little mad, she'd thought later. A lot mad. But now... For tonight there was no thought but their mutual need, no thought but the fire that was consuming them both. There were no words, no laughter, just burning, searing need that could only...must only...have one end.

Tina's breasts were twin peaks of want. Her body was arching, and still her mouth was locked onto Jock's. Their tongues were moving backwards and forwards, seeking, searching and devouring, and the want in their mouths was echoed and magnified a thousand times in their loins.

'Oh, God, Tina, I want you.'

It was the only thing Jock said, and that was a harsh, passionate whisper that she hardly heard. It was the only thing he needed to say, and even that was superfluous. They were gloriously naked by now, skin against skin, fire meeting fire, and Jock was over her, poised, and Tina was arching...up...up...her body pleading...

If he didn't come into her she'd surely die of wanting.

Then he entered her. Magically, wondrously, he entered her, descending straight into her like an arrow into fire, into the moist recesses between her thighs. The joy was indescribable. Jock's body was filling the dreadful emptiness of the night. He was uniting their two bodies as firmly—more firmly—than any wedding vow could ever do, making two into one.

As Tina felt him inside her, the last of her reason—the last of her sanity—disappeared on the soft night air. There was no reason in this, but this was where she wanted to be. All her life she had been waiting to feel like this, and she hadn't known it until now. She hadn't known a man's body could feel like this, could smell like this, could taste like this.

Tina's hands linked urgently around Jock's broad shoulders and she held him down to her, held him into her. This was her man, her heart. Her body arched and arched again, sending messages of love and desire and pure animal passion straight back to him.

The glorious rhythm began. Over and over he drove into her, drowning his need in her loveliness. Down... further and further, deeper and deeper into her body, deeper into her soul.

There was only Jock. Nothing else in the world could matter at all but this man and his body. The horror of the night receded to a dreadful blur that was now far away, a horror that could be assuaged by love. Anything in the world could be faced with this love, with Jock inside her.

'Jock... Jock...'

Whether she called his name out loud she didn't know, she didn't care. Maybe it was her voice, or maybe it was just her heart, but the word was a vow as binding as any marriage vow. Jock...

Jock.

Then the night exploded into a blur of love and mist and stars, and there was nothing, nothing but Jock. Nothing but the link between this man and this woman.

And nothing could ever be the same again.

'Coffee?'

Tina opened one eye and peered up at a world that was way too bright.

The morning sun was flooding in from the beach. From the bedroom windows there was a view straight down to the waves for the house was practically on the beach and the French windows opened to sand and sea beyond.

Tina winced at the brilliant light and glittering water. She rolled over in the bed—to find Jock standing in the doorway.

The rat was fully dressed. Dressed! Jeans, open-necked shirt and bare feet, but dressed for all that, and grinning like the cat that had caught the very fattest canary.

Tina hauled the bedclothes up to her neck and glared.

'What gives you the right to be so damned decent, Jock Blaxton?'

'I like playing superior.' Jock crossed to the bed and bent to give her a light kiss on the nose. 'I know I don't *need* to play superior—I am already—but you'll just have to indulge my whims. Being up and dressed and bringing breakfast to naked women in my bed is one of my very favourite pastimes.'

Whoa...

Tina flinched. Naked women... Just how many naked women was he talking here?

Keep it light, she told herself desperately, keep it as light as Jock wanted. Last night she had bared her soul to this man. She'd told him how she felt. She'd told him she loved him.

If he wanted her on those terms...well, it was over to him now. She couldn't say it again, she had to play it his way.

'Are you feeling better, then?' She managed a smile and reached out a hand gratefully for the coffee.

'Is that what last night was all about?' Jock asked, settling his long body onto the bed beside her, putting his hand into her riot of curls and letting his fingers drift. 'Making me feel good?'

'Of course.' Her eyes laughed up at him and her hand reached out to the crotch of his jeans and gently kneaded. 'Did I succeed?'

'Did you succeed?' He groaned and hauled back the bedclothes, nearly spilling her coffee in the process. She shoved the mug on the bedside table as his mouth went straight to the valley below her breasts and he kissed her just above her heart. Who could drink coffee with this happening?

'You can't imagine how you succeeded,' he told her. 'Or how awful I felt before you came.' Jock hesitated and gently started stroking the flatness of her belly, sending shivers from her toes right up her body and back again. And then some!

Then his voice grew serious, and his arms held her as if he was still seeking comfort.

'I don't know how you can work full time in a casualty department,' he told her. 'That's why I chose obstetrics. So I don't have to handle catastrophes like that every day.'

'You still get tragedies in obstetrics.' Tina twisted her fingers in his hair and stroked, but at the same time she was trying hard to hold herself aloof from the seductive tenderness of his arms. A little bit aloof so that when he put her away from him—as put her away he must—she could still continue. Naked *women*, he'd said. Remember that! Women, plural!

But Tina had no power in her to resist this man, naked women plural or not. Her fingers sifted through and through his thick black curls, holding his head to her heart, and every moment she was falling deeper and deeper in love with him. 'And… And I can't take tragedies alone either,' she whispered.

'That's why you came last night? Because you didn't want to be alone?'

Had he forgotten that she'd told him she loved him? Tina thought bleakly. Did he think it had been just a line—something she said to all her other lovers, the same way he reacted to all his other naked women…?

But… Despite how she felt, she couldn't say it again. She couldn't say the words 'I love you'.

The words had been right last night. It had been needful to make him love her last night and their emotional need had been raw, but this morning it would be blackmail to throw her emotional dependence on him.

'That's right,' she said, and if her voice was a little stiff he didn't appear to notice. 'That's why I came. I couldn't go home to Christie. Not after that.'

'Speaking of Christie, won't she be worried now?' Jock glanced sideways at his watch and then went back to what he was concentrating on—drawing circles with his fingers on the bare skin right above her navel, and then below. The sensation was driving her wild. 'Tina, it's nine on a Sunday morning,' he said softly. 'You don't think she'll fret when she wakes and you're not home?'

'I'm twenty-eight years old and last night I went out with a very attractive single man,' Tina said. Dear heaven, if he didn't stop stroking her there she'd just die! Or maybe she'd die if he did stop stroking. 'If she can't guess where I am then she's a dingbat. And Christie's not a dingbat.'

'I see.'

But he didn't, Tina knew. He was thinking... He was thinking she always did this. Slept with her dates. Said she loved them and threw herself at them. Good grief! She was no virgin, but...

'I guess...I guess I should go home now,' Tina said in a brittle, strained voice, 'and see if I can get a bit more sleep. I'm on duty tonight.'

'Do you have to go?'

'I should...' But Jock's hand was still doing its magic stroking and Tina's resolution was turning to melted butter.

'Tina..'

'Yes?'

Jock's mouth was following his fingers, his lips leaving a trail of kisses downwards from her breasts, and she was burning up all over again.

'It might have been a mistake for me to get dressed,' he admitted, in a voice husky with passion. 'Hell, Tina. Last night was our last date. Does it have to finish already?'

And, of course, it didn't.

But as Tina lay in her lover's arms an hour later, and waited for the day to start and the world to overtake them, she felt cold and sick to the core.

Because Jock's voice had been firm and sure.

'Our last date,' he'd said, and his voice had been absolutely sure.

Tina left at eleven and Jock went swimming. He swam for close on two hours, back and forth across the bay as if his life depended on it, trying to burn off some of this damned energy. Some of this damned restlessness.

God, she was lovely. What would it be like to have her in his bed every night for the rest of his life?

'So, what are you proposing here, Jock, boy?' he growled into the surf. 'Marriage? Kids? The full catastrophe? That's disaster country and you know it. You're already playing the fool. Hell, Jock, you didn't even take precautions last night.'

He'd asked her about that. As she'd showered and dressed in a borrowed shirt over her tattered bridesmaid's dress, he'd brought it up with some trepidation.

'Tina, last night... I didn't even think. I should have worn a condom, but things just got out of hand. Do we...? Are you...?'

'It's OK.' Tina's voice from under the shower had sounded strained and tired. Flat. 'It's the wrong time of the month, and even if it wasn't there's always the morning-after pill. I'm a big girl, Jock Blaxton. I can take care of myself. So relax—unless you've got something nasty I should know about?'

She'd made a joke of it, for which he was grateful, but it could have been a catastrophe. He did not want to go down that road. Pregnancy? No way! So why had he let his hold on his senses slip?

It had been the night, he told himself, and the horror.

But it was more than that. There had been this indescribable urge this morning... When he'd walked into the bedroom with her coffee and seen Tina, lying gloriously naked and fast asleep in his bed with her wonderful hair sprayed across the pillows... Her body... Her lovely body...

He'd wanted her so much it had hurt, and to let her go, without making love to her again, had been impossible. There'd been an urge to hold her to him for ever.

But that was the way of madness. It meant misery, as his father had known and as his father had taught his son to expect. He had to let her go. He must. He didn't want to get any more involved than he already was.

Damn, he was too involved now.

So... He'd never given Tina false promises, he told himself bleakly. She'd known from the start he didn't want to get involved. From now on the relationship must be purely professional, he told himself as he swam on.

'And, Jock, boy, if I were you I'd contact London tomorrow about that job. Because the sooner you get out of this place and remember your resolutions the better for all concerned.'

'You slept with Jock Blaxton?'

Christie eyed her sister's extraordinary outfit with stupefaction. One wrecked, bloodied bridesmaid's dress with one man's shirt over the top. She looked like something out of a horror movie. 'Good grief, Tina. Your dress is ripped all up the back. He didn't rape you?'

'Rape...? Why on earth...? Of course not.'

'There's blood on your dress. And it's in tatters.'

'Oh, yeah...' Tina looked down at her bridesmaid's dress and grimaced. 'Oh, heck.' She shook her head and managed a smile. 'No, Christie, he didn't rape me. It's been one hell of a night, and I'll tell you about it soon, but...'

Despite the horror of the night before—soon she would have to find the courage to tell Christie about it— Tina couldn't quite keep a tiny note of pleasure from her voice as she said the words. The night hadn't been all horror. 'I slept with Jock all of my own accord.'

'Well, well...' Christie shook her head in disbelief and hauled her baby closer to her breast. It was lunchtime for Rose and Rose was only interested in one thing. The love life of Aunty Tina was a matter of supreme indifference to young Rose Maiden. 'Well, well,' Christie said again, a little smile playing at the edges of her mouth. 'Does that mean Rose's Aunty Tina has found herself a decent man for a change?'

'What do you mean, a decent man?'

'Peter's a wimp,' Christie said bluntly. 'A cheque book on legs, and you can't say that about your Dr Blaxton. He's testosterone on legs. I don't know if he has money but it doesn't matter. He's not just a cheque book.'

'No.' Tina managed a smile as she shook her head. 'I guess you can't say he's just a cheque book, and I'd have to agree with the testosterone. But he's not *my* Dr Blaxton, Christie.'

'What do you mean?' Christie's eyes narrowed and she subjected her sister to a searching glance, seeing the troubled look behind Tina's smile. 'You *did* sleep with him. Tina, one-night stands are hardly your style.'

Tina had to agree. 'No.' She shook her head. 'They're not but, sadly, they're all Jock wants. And if a one-night stand is all I can have of Jock...' She spread her hands in resignation. 'Well, Christie, I'm taking crumbs! Or I've taken crumbs. I don't think Jock has any more to give.'

The repercussions of the accident on the night of the wedding blasted outwards through the valley with an almost shattering force, and the valley doctors were frantically busy for the next week. In a small community everyone was affected by such a tragedy.

The trauma was deep and far-reaching, and guilt and sorrow showed itself in all sorts of ways—from severe angina in an elderly uncle to a teenager presenting with eczema from head to toe. It didn't make any sense at all, but with sedation and counselling the eczema eased and so did the angina. Stress had inexplicable ways of showing itself.

The week finished with the teenage driver of the car attempting suicide, by which time the valley doctors were close to desperation themselves. Tina found herself so busy she hardly had time to think about Jock.

Hardly.

She didn't actively think about him—she was too busy to do that—but Jock was in the back of her thoughts all the time, a constant, overriding presence. Tina's life had been changed for ever, whether Jock was aware of it or not. Tina was absolutely, irrevocably, in love, absolutely, irrevocably, committed, no matter what Jock intended to do with that love.

Nothing, Tina thought bleakly as the awful week wore on and she saw nothing of Jock at all, he intends to do nothing. He's finished with me. Now he'll move on to the next of his two-date stands.

Ellen eyed her at the end of the week as she finished her shift. It was dawn, the time when human defences were at their weakest. Ellen bided her time—the girl looked just plain exhausted after a hectic night of duty and Ellen had been eyeing her sideways all night—and finally she pounced.

'Dr Rafter, are you going to tell Aunty Ellen what's going on here?' she asked.

'What do you mean?'

'I mean between you and Dr Blaxton.'

'Then no. I'm not saying a word.' Dawn or not, Tina wasn't stupid. She was adjusting a drip in a baby she'd admitted during the night with dehydration, and her fierce concentration wasn't solely to avoid Ellen's eyes. A tummy upset in a two-month-old baby could lead to death if the fluids weren't maintained, and little Brie had been losing fluids for twelve hours now. 'Ellen, I need electrolytes done here.'

'I've already ordered them.' Ellen moved her ample body around to block the door to the nursery as Tina turned to leave. There was a glint of resolution behind her glasses. 'Now, Tina, lass, you've been wandering round, looking miserable, ever since the night of the crash. I thought it was just the horror and then young Andrew's attempt at suicide...'

'It is.'

'It's not,' Ellen said firmly. 'You've coped magnificently with everything, and as for the grief…well, we've all had to go through that. But, Tina, you've coped with hysterical relatives and stomach pumps and the lot. You've counselled the kids who survived and you've done it well. The horror's fading—but the shadows under your eyes are getting darker.'

'I don't know what you mean.'

'It wouldn't be Dr Blaxton's announcement that he's leaving, would it?' Ellen demanded—and watched her.

'Leaving?' Tina's eyes flew to Ellen's. 'Oh, Ellen…'

'I wondered if you'd heard.' Ellen's eyes softened at the look of pain that washed across Tina's face. 'I was right, then. I thought as much. The man's been avoiding you all week and—'

'Avoiding me?'

'I watched you both last night,' Ellen said softly. 'Dr Blaxton delivered a baby and he had to come in here afterwards and check her—but you were in here, working on this little one. I heard him come down the corridor and had a bet with myself that he'd be distracted when he saw you were here, and sure enough…the man stopped at the door, saw you and left again. He decided to go find himself a cup of coffee. He came back an hour later when you were gone.'

'Ellen…'

'If you think it's natural that he stays up an hour longer just to have a cup of coffee in the middle of the night, I don't,' Ellen said solidly. 'You and I are on night shift and we go home now and to bed. Dr Blaxton is due to start his day in about an hour—but it's my bet he won't start until five minutes after you leave.'

'Ellen…'

'I'm not imagining it, am I?' Ellen went on mercilessly. 'There's things going on here between the pair of you. And now Dr Blaxton tells me that he's starting a new job in London as soon as Gina and Struan get back.'

Ellen's kindly eyes perused her young friend's face. 'He looks as bleak as you do, Dr Rafter,' she said softly. 'So...'

'So nothing.' Tina shrugged. 'So nothing, Ellen. You're imagining things. There's nothing between us.'

'Except?'

'Except nothing.'

There had to be nothing. If Jock was leaving for London then there had to be nothing. Except...

CHAPTER NINE

EXCEPT she was pregnant.

Tina was staring with horror at two blue lines. Then she shook the strip of lined plastic, as if somehow it could possibly be wrong. Somehow.

She wasn't wrong. The two lines stayed firmly blue. Immutable and absolute. One positive pregnancy test. Oh, no.

Tina sat back on her bed and stared down sightlessly at her lap. She'd suspected this. For the last week she'd been telling herself she was crazy. Sure, she was tired and her breasts were sore but, then, she'd been working too hard, she'd been disturbed a few times by Ally and Tim when she was supposed to be sleeping during the day, and her period was due. That was why her breasts were tender.

Only now... As of last Monday her period had been overdue and the tenderness in her breasts was increasing. So, telling herself all the time that she was stupid, there was no need to worry and that she was overreacting, she'd popped a pregnancy test in her bag and brought it home.

To this.

Dear God... What now? One thing was for sure, Jock wouldn't want to know about this. It had been nearly four weeks since the night she'd slept with Jock, and in those four weeks Jock had scarcely spoken to her. Their conversation had been limited to professional need, and she'd heard he'd taken out Sister Jackson, the sister in charge of the nursing home. Twice.

Had Sister Jackson turned into the next of Jock's naked women? Tina thought bleakly. Who knew? If she had then Jock would have moved on to the next lady by now. Tina turned numbly back to the strip of plastic and stared, willing the second line to go away. It didn't. The blue line seemed to be carved in stone. The test said that she, Tina Rafter, was one hundred per cent pregnant.

How could she have been so stupid? It had been the wrong time, she thought desperately, her period had barely finished on the night she'd slept with Jock. She shouldn't have ovulated for at least a week after that, she should have been safe. She couldn't possibly be pregnant. She was.

'Never discount pregnancy,' she heard the echoes of her old obstetric professor intoning. 'Even in a nunnery, never discount pregnancy. Sperm has a way of getting through walls three feet thick. It gets through vows of chastity and through pills and condoms and vasectomies. There's no known hundred per cent successful birth control method for a fertile woman except abstinence, and even abstinence has to be strongly suspect.'

Dear God.

She should have taken the morning-after pill. She should have—but, then, in the days after the crash she'd been frantically busy, and taking the morning-after pill…well, she'd had no samples. She would have needed to walk into the pharmacy and say to Horrible Kevin, the pharmacist of the sweaty hands and big mouth, 'please, I need a morning-after pill' and handed over a script written to herself. Kevin would have looked at her and smirked, and spread the word…

'This is stupid,' she told herself fiercely. 'It was your damned pride that stopped you asking for a morning-after pill. You know you should have. It was dumb stupidity. And now…'

Now what? Abortion?

Unconsciously Tina's hand dropped to her abdomen.

It was flat and tight and hard, but the blue line told her that somewhere in there a tiny life was stirring—a life created by the love between Jock and Tina, a life created by their mutual need.

Only Jock no longer needed her—he'd moved on.

'It's just a foetus,' Tina said aloud, as if calling it the hard anatomical name would make it less than it really was. 'A foetus, not a baby. It's no bigger than a tadpole. And it's going to wreck your life. You're only five weeks pregnant, you can abort…'

No.

No. The word slammed into her heart and it stayed there. Unwittingly her hands formed a link across her stomach and held, in the age-old gesture of a woman protecting what was most precious to her.

She had turned twenty-nine last week. Twenty-nine.

'I'm twenty-nine years old and I'm going to have a baby,' she whispered, and suddenly it didn't seem such a disaster. Suddenly there was joy flooding through the terror, and the link of her hands across her stomach grew tighter. A baby…

How could she get rid of a baby that was part of her and part of the man she loved? she asked herself.

She couldn't. No way! No matter what Jock wanted, this baby had been created with love, it was here to stay—and she'd welcome it with joy. As for the practicalities…

There was a knock on the door and her sister peered around, her face anxious. Baby Rose was in Christie's arms, and Ally and Tim were stalking behind.

'You've been in here for ages,' Christie said. 'Is there something wrong?'

'Maybe. Maybe not.' Tina took a deep breath. She had to start some time; she had to plan for a future here, a future for all of them. 'Christie, you know…you know I said that I'd only stay here for a few months?'

'Yes?' Christie was no longer watching Tina. Her eyes were on the little piece of plastic, lying on her sister's lap, and the box it came in beside her on the bed. PREGTEST, the label on the box said in demure blue letters, the blue the same colour as the two blue lines on the plastic.

'I...I think I might be staying longer,' Tina said, and her voice shook. 'Christie...' She looked up at her big sister and the tables were suddenly turned. For the past two months she'd cared for Christie, hauling her slowly out of her well of depression, but it was Christie who was the strong one now. It was Christie who gathered her little sister in a bear hug and held her close, with Rose somehow squashed between them. 'Oh, Christie.' She gulped on a sob of fright. 'How on earth will we manage with four babies between us?'

'You have to tell him.'

Four cups of tea later, Christie and Tina were still staring at each other over the table. The change in Christie was astounding. If any good was coming of this, it was starting with Christie, Tina thought wryly. The dejected woman who'd had trouble raising a smile and who'd been content to let Tina and Marie run her life had disappeared. Now she was taking up cudgels; she was going to war on Tina's behalf—and she'd love doing it.

'Jock has a responsibility here, Tina, he made you pregnant. He'll have to pay child maintenance at the very least.'

'I guess.' Tina stirred her tea and looked sightlessly into its depths. 'I did tell him I was safe. I can't hold him...'

At the look on her face, Christie hesitated.

'Tina, are you so sure there's nothing left between you?' she probed gently, changing tack from anger to sympathy. 'Nothing that can be salvaged? I mean…you and Jock. You make a lovely couple. He'd make a lovely husband.'

'No.' Tina put down her mug with a thump. 'That's one thing he wouldn't, Christie. He makes a wonderful doctor and he makes a good friend. And…' Her face turned pink. 'And he also makes a great lover. The best. But Jock will make no woman a husband—he's vowed that all along. He slept with me with no promises at all and now he's taking out someone else. He doesn't want this baby, Christie, and he doesn't want me.'

'But you'll still tell him you're pregnant?'

'I think I must,' Tina said bleakly. 'He is the…he is my baby's father, and when he goes…' Tina's voice faltered. Jock was leaving for London and there was nothing she could do about it. 'When he goes away to London,' she said slowly, 'he needs to know he's leaving a little part of him behind.'

'He's leaving his baby.' Christie's voice softened almost to a whisper. 'Oh, Tina, what if he wants it? What if he wants to be a daddy?'

'I don't think there's any chance of that,' Tina told her sister, and her voice was bleak. 'One baby too many… Boy, there surely is one baby too many now.'

'She went to sleep before tea and woke up hungry so I made her a peanut-butter sandwich. She ate it and suddenly…suddenly…'

Midnight, a peaceful night in Casualty—until now. The woman's voice was hoarse with terror. She was standing in the entrance to Casualty, holding her toddler in her arms and clutching her close in fear. She wouldn't release her, and it took all of Tina's strength to prise the woman's arms away so she could see the child.

And the child was in deadly trouble.

At a silent, urgent eye message from Tina, Barbara,

the casualty sister, came forward and took Mrs Hughes's arm, pulling her gently aside but brooking no argument.

'Let her be, Mrs Hughes. Let Dr Rafter examine her.'

But Claire Hughes was past reason. She started to sob, a harsh, piercing sob that racked her whole body, and she pulled away from Barbara in terror.

'She's dying. She's dying... I had to leave the other children with the neighbour. My husband's at work and I couldn't find... Oh, dear God...'

'Claire...'

Claire wasn't listening. She had a hysterical personality at the best of times, and this was the worst. The woman slumped forward, crumpling to the floor in over-blown passion, and grabbed Tina by the leg.

'My baby. My baby. My baby...'

The baby was turning blue. Tina looked down at the child, trying to balance against the woman hauling at her leg and hold the child and see at the same time. She didn't need to see much—Tina knew instantly what was happening.

The mother had said she'd eaten a peanut-butter sandwich. Peanuts. It must be the peanuts. The child's whole body was swelling. Her eyes were puffy, swollen slits and there was an angry red rash over her arms and face. Her breathing was shallow and painful and...

Suddenly, the breathing was non-existent, and through her sobs Claire heard the breathing stop.

She screamed, grabbed Tina's other leg and tried to drag her down with her.

'No. No. No!'

'Let me go.' Tina hauled herself backwards but the woman still held on. 'Mrs Hughes, let me go!' Tina pulled back with all her strength, but her arms were full of unconscious toddler. The nursing sister bent over to try and take the woman away, but Claire lashed out. She was way beyond reason, way beyond thought.

'Claire!' The harsh, male voice shot out over the room, catching them all. Jock had been passing the door. One glance in had told him what was going on, and three fast strides took him to Claire.

He asked no questions. He lifted the woman bodily into his arms, hauled her away from Tina and dumped her unceremoniously in a chair beside the door.

'Stay there and don't you move an inch,' he snapped, in a voice that would have stopped an army in its tracks. 'Barbara, stay with her and don't let her move. Call Security if you must. Tina, bring the little one in here.' He held the door of the examination cubicle wide and Tina practically ran in. A flick of the lock and the hysterical mother was Barbara's concern, safely locked on the other side of the door. At last they could concentrate on what was happening. The child was still not breathing, and the awful blue was fading to a ghastly white.

'Intubation,' Tina gasped. 'There's no time...'

The child's throat must have swollen completely shut. There was no way they could do artificial resuscitation without a tube. There was no room for the air to get through the swollen throat and there was no time for antihistamine to work. But Tina didn't have to tell Jock what was needed. Before she'd settled the toddler onto the couch Jock was at the crash cart, sorting out what he needed. It took him seconds.

He moved like lightning. One fast swipe of lubricant on the intubation tube and he'd turned back while Tina was still lowering the little one onto her back, tilting her head and lifting her jaw. They moved like two parts of a whole. As the tube was readied Jock deferred to Tina. She was the anaesthetist, and she had the skills to intubate. He took over positioning the jaw so Tina could insert the laryngoscope and carefully, carefully, position the tube.

The vocal chords were so swollen…

Jock tilted the jaw further, his hands rock-steady, and Tina slid the tube down. Almost before she had the tube in place Jock was moving again, injecting adrenalin. Before she needed to ask he'd readied the bag for ventilation. In seconds—less—they had it connected. Then, as Tina breathed gently into the limp little body, Jock started to set up the IV line for antihistamine. Dear God, let them be in time…

One puff of the ventilator bag. Another and then another. Please… And then the child took one long harsh, grating breath, and the little chest moved of its own accord. Tina practically sagged in relief.

Medicine! Who'd be a doctor? she thought grimly as the child started to breathe again. One minute she'd been sitting having a coffee with Barbara and the next she'd been fighting for a little life.

She held the tube carefully in place, mindful of the child's natural reaction before they had the chance to sedate. Without sedation she'd gag on the tube. But Jock was already organising antihistamine and sedation. She may well have lost this life without Jock, Tina acknowledged. With an uncontrolled, hysterical mother on her hands and with a baby not breathing…

Peanuts, Tina thought bitterly as she and Jock worked on to stabilise the little one's breathing. Ban all peanuts! They were so dangerous. Hardly anyone knew how allergenic they could be—except the people who reacted like this.

Little Marika Hughes would be fine now, but she'd spend the rest of her life being careful about her food, reading ingredients, and carrying adrenalin and antihistamine wherever she went because there were foods made with compounds of ingredients where peanuts weren't listed.

There was a knock on the door and there was time

now for Tina to answer it. Barbara stood there, her face creased in concern. One look at little Marika's face, fast regaining its colour, and Barbara's own face flushed.

'Oh, thank God. She'll be OK?'

'I think so.' Tina managed a shaky smile. They had come so close... She gestured to Jock who was still working. They'd keep the tracheotomy tube in place for several hours until the last of the swelling had gone down. The toddler would have to be sedated to hold it in. Still, that was the least of their problems now. 'How's her mum?' she asked. 'Quieter?'

'I had to knock her out,' Barbara said. 'I'm sorry. There was no other doctor in the hospital, and as soon as you guys locked yourselves away she went bananas. More bananas. She kicked Eric right where it hurt most, and if we hadn't stopped her she would have broken this door down.'

Tina grimaced. Thank heaven Eric, their security guard, was large.

'What did you give her?'

'Valium intramuscularly. Eric held her down while I gave it to her. Oh, and her husband arrived and he helped administer it.' Barbara nursed a bruised arm. 'She'll probably have us all up for assault.'

'You may well be able to put in a counter-charge.' Tina frowned down at the ugly bruise on Barbara's arm. 'Are you OK?'

'Yeah, well, I'll live. And I won't do that—she really was terrified.' She hesitated. 'The husband's still here,' she added, with another look at Marika. 'Do you have time to talk to him? He's going out of his tree—only not so volubly as his wife.'

Tina flashed a glance at Jock. His hands were still working on the IV line. He had such skilled hands, Tina thought inconsequentially. And his face...

He did love babies, Tina thought, and the idea was

like a kick in the stomach. He did. And he *should* want them. He *should* want babies of his own.

He should want a wife, too, but he didn't, and now... Now, like it or not, Jock's child would be coming into the world, and he wouldn't want to know about it.

'I...I'll come back in a few minutes, Jock,' Tina said aloud, and if her voice shook surely it was because of the tension of the last few minutes. Surely! 'If you can stay with her...'

'I'll stay.'

He would—she hadn't needed to ask. Wild horses couldn't have dragged Jock away from a baby whose life was on the line. So how would he react to a baby of his own?

It was half an hour before Tina found Jock again. She'd had to calm Barry Hughes, reassure him that things were OK and then see to his wife. They'd settled her in a single room and Tina wrote her up for admission overnight. Barry had more children at home and he had enough on his plate, without sending Claire home with him.

Now she had to write up retrospective orders for drugs. In theory, Barbara had no business giving drugs without doctors' orders. In practice it had been a choice of drugging her or calling the police and having her dragged away, screaming.

Now... Claire was close to sleep, medicated almost to oblivion. She was tucked firmly into bed, with metal guard rails on either side of the bed to keep her safe and a junior nurse in attendance. She managed to open her eyes as Tina came in, and kept them wide long enough to get out her most important question.

'I'm... Oh... Marika...'

'Marika's safe,' Tina said firmly, crossing to take the woman's hand. 'She's fine. She's fast asleep. Dr Blaxton is looking after her and the swelling's already going down. You'll see her in the morning, but she really is OK.'

'Oh, Marika... Oh, I'm so sorry...'

The woman let a weary tear slide down her face, and then slid into sleep.

Jock was sitting in the children's ward with Marika when Tina went to find him. He was alone. Barry had been and gone—home to care for his two other small children. The man had a heavy weight on his shoulders, Tina thought—three tiny children and a wife who reacted to emergencies with hysterics was no one's idea of a picnic.

This could well have been fatal. If it hadn't been for Jock...

Tina stood at the door of the darkened ward and watched him for a couple of moments before she entered. Unaware of her presence, Jock sat. He was totally still, calm and watchful, his total attention on watching the gentle rise and fall of the little one's chest.

It was as if he wasn't tired in the least, Tina thought. It was as if he had nothing better to do in the whole world than to watch the steady breathing of this child. He loved. He was a man capable of so much love...

Unconsciously, Tina's hand dropped to her abdomen and fleetingly stayed there. She was eight weeks pregnant. In five more weeks Jock was due to leave—to take himself off to the other side of the world. Would he ever look down at his own child with the same tenderness with which he was watching this little one?

No way. One baby too many... But she had to tell him, and there was no easy way.

'Jock?'

Jock glanced up and smiled, but his smile was abstracted. His attention was only on his little patient. There was no way he would focus his attention on Tina, not now. She'd had her allotted two dates with this man. Jock had moved on.

'She's fine,' he said softly, turning back to the bed. 'The nurse will come in soon and take over obs but I thought I'd sit here for a bit, just to make sure she's stabilised. There's no need for you to stay.'

She was dismissed. There was no mistaking the finality of his tone. He didn't want her here, but Tina had something to say. It had to be said, and there was never going to be a better time than now—in this darkened room and in the intimacy of a shared success—in the time before the world broke in again.

All she needed was courage, a trainload of courage. She needed the courage to ignore the dismissal and say what she needed to say—to say what he least wanted to hear, what he'd spent a lifetime avoiding. She took a deep breath, wiped her suddenly moist palms on the sides of her white coat and crossed to sit on the chair on the other side of the toddler's bed.

'Jock, I need to talk to you,' she said, and her voice gave a definite wobble. 'I need—'

'Do you have a medical problem?' There it was again. The blunt, harsh dismissal. Medicine or nothing.

'In a way.' Courage, Tina, courage. She tilted her chin and met Jock's look head-on over the bedclothes. The only sound was the faint whistle of Marika's breathing through the tube—nothing else.

'I'm pregnant.'

Then there was nothing, no sound at all. It went on and on, the silence stretching into a minute. Two minutes. Three. Finally Tina could bear it no longer. Jock's face was totally impassive, and he sat like a man carved in stone. There was no warmth at all in his look, nothing except blankness. Say something, Tina's heart screamed, say something, but he said nothing at all. She couldn't bear it. She couldn't. So... Where did she go

from here? She didn't know, but wherever she went Tina
knew she would be travelling alone. She'd said what
she'd had to say, and now she had to leave.

'I'll...I'll leave you to it. I need to go back to
Casualty.' Tina finally found the strength to rise to her
feet. One more look at that cold face and she shuddered
and turned away. There was pain shooting through and
through her. It was a pain worse than any physical agony.

Dear God, she loved this man, but he wanted nothing
to do with her—nothing to do with her or with his child.
'I'm sorry, Jock,' she whispered, 'but I thought you
ought to know.' And she turned and walked straight out
of the room.

One of the night nurses was just coming in as she
left—Penny, the nurse who was taking over Marika's
obs from Jock. She smiled at Tina and then turned in
astonishment to watch as Tina walked straight past her.
There was no answering smile, nothing, as Tina made
her way blindly along the corridor toward Cas.

Tina was known for her laughter and her friendliness
and her bounce. There was no bounce in her tonight.
Something dreadful must have happened. Fearfully the
nurse walked on, swinging open the door of the children's ward and expecting the worst. Sister Silverton had
told her that little Marika Hughes was recovering, but
by the look on Dr Rafter's face she expected to be walking in on a dead baby.

She wasn't. Marika Hughes was sleeping soundly and
breathing steadily—it was a good result. But Dr
Blaxton... Penny stared down at him in amazement for
Dr Blaxton had the same look on his face as Tina had
had. It was a look the young nurse had never seen before, and Penny had been out with him twice.

'Thanks, Penny,' Jock said blankly. He rose and
stretched his long frame, but the look on his face didn't

alter. 'Don't leave her alone for a minute,' he ordered, handing over the chart. 'Ten-minute blood-pressure checks, keep an eagle eye on that tube and give me a ring the minute there's any change. But I don't expect there to be. The swelling's reducing already so I'll leave you to it.'

He walked out of the room in the same trance-like state in which the nurse had just seen Tina.

CHAPTER TEN

TINA was writing patient histories when Jock arrived. Her red curls were falling over her face, her head was bent and she was concentrating fiercely on what she was doing. She was concentrating as if it was the most important thing in the world to record what had happened to Marika Hughes on this night.

Sister Roberts was cleaning the examination cubicle at the far end of Casualty. The door to the cubicle was closed so, working in a pool of light in the dimmed casualty area, Tina seemed totally isolated. Jock felt his heart wrench. Dear heaven, she was so alone, and she was so lovely. She was pregnant with his child.

How was he supposed to feel? he wondered. He stood in the entrance and stared across at this enigmatic child-woman, this laughing, lovely creature who'd bewitched him from the moment he'd seen her, and he felt the old irrational fears surge through and through him. And some!

Tina. Pregnant.

He hadn't wanted this. He hadn't! How could she possibly be pregnant? How was he supposed to cope with this? But Tina was bent over her work and her hair was falling forward and... Dear God, he loved her. But hell! Pregnant!

He was going to London, he thought savagely. Leaving. The job overseas had been confirmed. He didn't want to be in love with anyone, he didn't want to feel like this about Tina and he didn't want to be a father to this child. He didn't want...

Tina looked up at him and smiled, and Jock's thoughts

stopped in mid-sentence. He didn't know what the hell he didn't want—or what he did want. In the last five minutes his orderly world had been turned upside down and the rules had all changed. Or maybe it had been turned upside down the minute Tina had walked into his life.

'It's OK, Jock,' Tina said steadily, the smile still on her face and the pain in her face almost hidden from the outside world. Almost. 'It's fine. There's no need to look like that.' God, was his panic so obvious? 'There's no call for you to marry me or worry about us or for you to have any part in this. I'm not holding you to me. I...I just thought...you have the right to know about the baby before you leave.'

'Tina, what the...?' With one explosive oath Jock was over the other side of the room, shoving his palms flat on her desk and bending forward to meet her head to head. 'What the hell is happening here? I don't understand. You told me you were safe. You told me you'd take precautions, and you're not stupid.'

'That's just it. I was stupid.'

'No. You're not a dope, Tina. If you're pregnant then you wanted to get pregnant.'

She didn't flinch, not outwardly at least.

'No, Jock, I didn't want to get pregnant,' she said steadily. 'No matter how it looks, I didn't set out to trap you. You have to believe that. I thought...I really did think it was the wrong time of the month. It was—but I should have made sure. I know no time is completely safe but it was just that...I couldn't bring myself to take the morning-after pill so maybe subconsciously... Maybe...'

She spread her hands, trying to make him see, trying to make sense of things herself.

'You see, to me this baby's not a disaster, Jock,' she managed.

'Not a disaster?' He stared down disbelievingly. 'Of course it's a disaster. It's a total, unmitigated disaster. On a scale of one to ten it ranks about a hundred and fifty. Of all the stupid, senseless...'

But Tina had had enough. These words meant nothing and she didn't want to hear them. *Stupid. Senseless.* This was a baby they were talking about here. A baby whose mother was Tina and whose father was Jock. A child. She rose and backed against the wall, standing as far away from him as she could without walking past him and leaving. Her hands knotted behind her back—a gesture of defence against the emotions flooding through her—and her face was deathly white.

Senseless? Jock's baby? No and no and no.

'Jock, I have to tell you...' She closed her eyes for a long moment, and when she opened them she knew exactly what she wanted to say. She needed to tell him what was in her heart. She needed to give him the truth, stupid or not—and let him do with it what he willed.

'Jock, my stupidity has nothing to do with this pregnancy,' she whispered. 'Not now. It's time to look forward, not back.'

'But—'

'No, just listen. Jock, I'm twenty-nine years old and I've fallen in love. Stupid or not, I've fallen totally, blindly, absolutely, in love with you. I'm more in love than I've ever been in my life. I've never felt this way about anyone and I've lived for twenty-nine years. But...you're leaving and I know...I know the odds on me feeling like this about anyone else are impossible. So the thought of carrying your baby fills me with joy.'

The hard incredulity was still on Jock's face. 'You mean you *did* want to get pregnant,' he said flatly.

'No.' Tina's voice was as flat as his. As hard. Negating his accusation. 'I didn't. But now that I am...I can no sooner have an abortion than I can fly. Unlike you, I don't think there's one too many babies in the world. I can care for this baby. I'll give this little one all my love. All my love...'

'You're broke,' Jock said bluntly, cruelly. 'How the hell do you intend to care for it?'

Tina's chin went up then. Practicalities she was good at; plans were what filled the void.

'Christie and I have talked about it. If Struan will give me a permanent job—and when I took the job he said he'd like me here permanently—then I'll stay in Gundowring. Christie will sell the farm, move into town and we'll live together. We'll manage—we don't need much. Christie will be at home while I work, and my wage will support us all.'

'You have it all planned.' Anger was riding through and through him as Jock watched Tina speak. They had it all worked out, these women, but where the hell did that leave him?

'Jock...'

'Why the hell?' He swore and turned away from her, staring bleakly out the window into the darkness. 'Hell, Tina, am I supposed to just walk away? Walk away from my child?'

'So what do you want to do?' she asked gently. 'What do you want to do with fatherhood, Jock?'

Silence. Nothing. Then Jock made a decision. It felt hard and leaden and dreadful—and flew against everything he had ever been taught. He felt trapped. But this was Tina. Hell, this was Tina! He'd walked right into this trap and maybe it was time to let the door swing shut and accept his fate.

'We'll have to get married,' Jock said heavily. 'I can't see anything else for it.'

'He proposed.'

'Yep.'

'Oh, Tina…'

'Now, before you start getting carried away and planning weddings, let's get one thing clear,' Tina told her sister. 'I am not marrying Jock. Pregnant or not, marriage is out of the question. There is no way I am trapping Jock into marriage.'

'But—'

'Christie, he said, "We'll have to get married. I can't see anything else for it." And he looked as sick as a horse.'

'Oh,' Christie said doubtfully, and her face fell. 'I see.'

'I knew *you* would, but *he* can't see it. He doesn't understand why I won't.'

'You mean he still wants—'

'He wants to be honourable,' Tina burst out. 'He wants a wife and baby like a hole in the head, but he's going to do the right thing by us, by golly. So now he'll marry me if he has to shove me down the aisle in front of a shotgun.'

'It's supposed to be the bride's father, shoving the groom down the aisle with a shotgun when you're in this condition,' Christie said dubiously. 'I don't think I've ever heard of a groom doing it with a bride.'

'Yeah, well, you're not about to see it now,' Tina told her. 'I told him to take his wedding and shove it.'

'And he said…'

'He said we'd talk about it tomorrow when we're more rational.'

'Oh.'

'"Oh" is right. Oh, no!'

'We'll get married on the seventh of November.'

'Pardon?'

It was seven o'clock the next night. Tina had been at work for a whole five minutes. She'd barely had time to put her white coat on and hang her stethoscope around her neck before Jock came striding through the doors.

'It's the first date that we can legally do it,' Jock said bluntly. 'I've checked. There's a month's cooling-off period, between applying for a licence and marrying.'

'I'm sorry.' Tina dug her hands deep into the pockets of her white coat and glared. 'You'll have to explain. I seem to have missed out on part of the conversation here.'

'Like?'

'Like the hero going down on bended knee and laying his heart on his sleeve. And the heroine—that's me, by the way—turning a blushing shade of rose and coyly saying, "Oh, really, Dr Blaxton, you'll have to ask my father".' She managed a shaky smile. 'And then the hero—that's you—producing a diamond worth enough to take my breath away and sweeping me into his arms and against his heart—for ever. I've read my romances, Dr Blaxton. I know what's what.'

'Don't be stupid.'

'You see, that's just it,' Tina said sadly. 'I am stupid. You said it yourself. Stupid to get myself pregnant. Stupid to be in this mess in the first place. Stupid even to love you. So you don't want a stupid bride, Dr Blaxton, you don't want a bride at all.'

'Tina...'

'You don't want to be married, Jock,' Tina said, and her voice was flat. 'And, baby or not, I'm not marrying any man who doesn't love me.'

Jock took a deep breath, steadying himself. 'Tina, that's blackmail.'

'Well, it's a strange kind of blackmail,' Tina snapped. 'There's a common misconception that love comes before marriage. I might love you, Jock Blaxton, but there is no way on this earth I am marrying you if you don't love me right back.'

'Tina…'

'I have a customer,' she said coldly, as a car swept into the entrance. 'Don't you have any babies to deliver?'

'Not at the moment.'

'Then go away and annoy someone else,' she told him. 'Or check out Sarah Page, the new nurse down on Two East. She's only been working here for two nights so maybe she's escaped your attentions so far. A whole new nurse, Dr Blaxton. That's two great evenings, seeing if you can make someone else fall in love with you before you leave for London. But go away. I'm working and I'm not interested in your crazy plans.'

He didn't go far away at all. Jock hovered, stopping to speak to the cas. sister before leaving, unsure whether to go or stay—unsure just what the heck to do. His head was spinning. Hell, she had to marry him. He couldn't leave now. But…

Then he paused as he saw Barbara, the cas. sister, helping a middle-aged man out of a car and onto a trolley at the entrance to Casualty. The man was naked from the waist up, bent double, unable to straighten. Tina was crossing quickly to see what the trouble was, and Jock figured he'd stick around and check he wasn't needed.

It beat going back to his lonely house with things still undecided. It beat letting himself think any more. There was a woman rushing from the driver's seat of the car to help the man onto the trolley, and Jock recognised her. It was Lorna Colsworth, head of Gundowring's ladies bowling team, member of the hospital board, upholder of the town's moral principles. Wife of the local undertaker, Simon Colsworth.

Jock glanced at the trolley, expecting to see Simon, but it wasn't Simon. It was Reg Carney, the town's butcher, red-faced, overweight and with his features contorted in agony. Lorna was nearly as red-faced as the

man on the trolley. She was carrying a heap of clothes—
a shirt, a jacket and tie, socks and shoes. These she practically threw into Jock's arms as he stepped forward.

'Here. Take these and give them to him when he...
when he... Look, I have to go. I can't...'

But Jock put his hand on Lorna's arm, and his grip,
although gentle, was suddenly far too strong for her to
break from.

'Lorna, what's wrong?' From where he stood, Jock
couldn't see what the problem was. Tina was bending
over the man on the trolley, trying to get him to speak.
The man looked almost beyond speech.

If he'd eaten something—poison maybe—or taken
drugs or been injured, it was imperative that Lorna told
all she knew before she left. She mustn't be allowed to
leave. She certainly was desperate to go.

'I don't... Look, I really have to get home. These are
his clothes...' She took a frantic step back but Jock's
grip tightened.

'Tell us, Lorna.' He glanced at Tina, who had given
up trying to get the man to speak and was now prising
his hands away from his groin. The man was moaning
in agony, swaying from side to side on the stretcher.
'What's wrong?'

'It's his... It's his...' Lorna's crimson colour was now
close to purple. She looked like she was about to suffer
a stroke all on her own, and Jock hauled her sideways
and propelled her onto a chair. He needed to know, but
he didn't want her dropping dead on them before she
could tell.

'Lorna! Tell me!'

Lorna groaned, and groaned again. 'It's his...his...his
willy,' she burst out, and her voice was an agonised
whisper. 'It's stuck. Oh, you have to let me go. Please...'

Jock swung back to Tina and stared, just as Tina managed to haul away the man's hands. Tina gazed down

and her jaw dropped. For one moment—a fleeting second only—Jock saw the creases of Tina's green eyes wrinkle upward in an involuntary choke of laughter, but she didn't make a sound. Somehow her laughter was caught and held, and Jock abandoned Lorna and stepped forward to see.

Reg was caught in the most invidious position known to man. His penis was stuck firmly in the zipper of his pants, the teeth of the zipper cutting into the foreskin, and underneath... Underneath the heavy twill of his pants, surrounding the penis, was a frothy, frilly scrap of red and white...knickers? It was embedded in the wound, cutting in. Reg must have hauled at the thing with force to make it cut in so deeply.

Tina touched it and shook her head in disbelief. 'What...?' She looked back to Lorna. 'Mrs Colsworth... Mrs Colsworth, what is this?'

'They're my panties,' Lorna groaned, and she covered her face with her hand. 'At least...Reg just gave them to me tonight, as a present. They're...they're crutchless knickers from one of those adults-only shops. It was just a bit of fun, like, and he bought them for me for a laugh.'

Her face was flushing from puce to white and back to puce again, but somehow she kept on speaking. 'But... we were fooling around and...and I made Reg put them on—just to see what he'd look like, you know, for a bit of a giggle—and we heard a car. We thought it was Simon coming home, even though it's his Masons' night, and Reg got such a fright. He grabbed his pants and hauled them on too fast and...and he caught...and we couldn't get... We tried, but he couldn't. Then I tried but he screamed almost loud enough for the neighbours to hear. And it wasn't even Simon—it was only someone coming next door.'

It was all too much. Lorna's voice died away into a humiliated sob.

'Hey.' Somehow Jock kept a straight face, though afterwards he could never figure out how. He'd never been so close to losing it in his life. 'Hey, Lorna...' He bent over the distressed woman and took her hands.

'I don't... I can't bear...'

'*You* can't bear?' Reg moaned from the trolley. '*You* can't bear...? It's *me* who's stuck in the dammed things, woman. You damned near hauled me dick off when you pulled. Get me out of here.'

'Lorna, go home,' Jock said gently. 'Now we know what's wrong we can fix this. Believe it or not, it's a fairly common accident. Go home and ring later to check that Reg is OK.'

'But...' Lorna looked wildly up at them. 'Simon... Everyone... They'll know. They'll all find out.'

'Dr Rafter, Sister Roberts and I will know,' Jock said firmly. 'But that's all. We promise that nothing...no information at all...will go out of this room. That's a promise, Lorna. We'll even burn the panties.' A muscle at the side of his face twitched but he managed, somehow, to keep it under control. 'They're too damaged for further...further use. Now go home and get yourself under control before this husband of yours does come home.'

'You mean...'

'Lorna, go.'

It took them twenty minutes to free Reg from his entrapment—nineteen minutes for them to calm the man down and stop him writhing long enough for Tina to inject a tiny amount of local anaesthetic, and one minute or less for Jock to put a tiny nick in the foreskin and pull the whole zip down.

The lacy confection ripped as he brought it down with the trousers. Tina and Jock helped the man off with his pants and what was left of his knickers, without saying a word. Tina handed them back to Barbara. Barbara choked and left swiftly, her face strangely still.

'Can I telephone someone to bring you in fresh clothes?' Tina asked, managing to keep a straight face with an almost superhuman effort.

'No!' The moment Jock had finished dressing the wound Reg staggered to his feet. 'I'm going home. Lend me one of them hospital gown things.'

'Wear a hospital gown home? What...?' Tina took a deep breath. 'What about your wife, then, Reg?'

'She's at cards,' Reg managed. 'I gotta get home before she does. Call me a cab...' Then he had second thoughts. 'No. The taxi driver... Hell, it'll be Ted Farndale. It'll be all over town if he finds out...'

'How did you get to Lorna's?' Jock asked curiously.

'Walked. It's only two blocks and I wasn't going to risk parking the car outside, now was I?'

'I suppose not,' Jock said gravely. Then he rose to the occasion, as all men did to support each other in times of greatest need. 'Come on, Reg,' he said, his dark eyes twinkling. 'I'll drive you home. I'm off duty here. We'll leave Dr Rafter to deal with any more emergencies that chance in tonight.' He lifted a hospital gown and helped Reg into it.

'But don't go away, Dr Rafter,' he said softly, so softly that only she could hear it. 'There are things you and I still have to settle. One marriage, for instance.'

CHAPTER ELEVEN

JOCK returned ten minutes later to find Tina writing
again. She looked up as he entered but this time there
was no strain. Her face was creased into a wide smile,
and Jock knew she'd been in a bubble of laughter ever
since he'd left.

'Did you get him all the way home, without anyone
seeing?' She grinned. 'I had thought of trying to rustle
up a false moustache and dark glasses.'

'He would have taken them if you had.' Jock's grin
matched hers. 'Boy, if those two are ever unfaithful
again I'll be a monkey's uncle—and how I'll buy my
sausages in future and keep a straight face...'

'Ditto.' Then Tina's smile faded a little. 'This may
have one good outcome, though.'

'Which is...?'

'Lorna Colsworth is one of the biggest prudes in this
town, and she's on the hospital board. As a single mum,
I'd expect a pretty hard time from Lorna. She may even
want me sacked, but I can't see her giving me a hard
time now—can you?'

Jock's smile died as if it had never been, died to nothing.

'Tina...'

'I've been trying to figure out what to put on Reg's
history,' Tina said, ignoring Jock's discomfort. 'It's
unethical, but maybe it'd be kinder not to include it at
all. If any doctor down the track asks him what this was
all about, he'd die of heart failure right there on the
spot.'

'Tina...'

'What do you think?'

'I think we need to talk.'

'I thought we were talking.'

'About us.'

Tina shook her head and bent over her work again. 'There's no "us", Jock. There's you and there's me and there's our baby, but there's no "us".'

'I think there must be.'

'Why?' Tina didn't lack courage. She met his look, her eyes defiant. 'To fulfil your obligations? I don't think so.' She shook her head. 'Jock, you don't want to marry me. Be honest and admit it—you don't.'

Jock stared down at her for a long minute, and then he sat heavily on the chair on the other side of the desk. This girl... She made him smile as no one else had ever made him smile. She made him feel like all he wanted to do in life was to be with her, laugh with her, love her. Protect her...

But...marriage?

'That's just it, Tina. I don't know what I want.'

'If you don't know then you don't want marriage.'

'Hell...' Jock ran his hand through his hair and stood. He walked to the other side of the ward and then returned to sit again. He raked his hair some more while Tina sat as still as a stone and looked on, trying hard to contain her churning emotions and keep her look sympathetic, interested but unemotional. The very opposite to how she was feeling.

Finally she laid down her pen and closed her eyes on his pacing, closed her heart. Enough was enough—she couldn't bear it any more.

'Jock, go home and go to bed,' she said softly. 'I have work to do and you're tired. Keep this until tomorrow. Don't let it disturb your sleep tonight.'

'Damn it!' Jock exploded, and his hand came crashing down on the desk, making Tina jump. 'Damn it, woman, is that all you can say? That I have work to do and you're tired? Keep this until tomorrow—as if it's a piece of your damned paperwork?'

'What am I supposed to say?'

'I have no idea, but...' Jock shook his head despairingly. 'Tina, this love thing. Hell...'

'It's not hell, Jock.'

'It is.' He swore. 'Love... It's something I've been trained since birth not to feel. Don't get close or you'll damage. You'll destroy, and be destroyed in turn. But it's crazy. Other people have happy marriages, just not my parents. They were the exception—not the rule—and it's time I learned that. So why can't I marry?'

'Do you want a happy marriage?'

'Yes... No! Tina, I don't know.' Jock looked over at her and his eyes were desperate. 'I only know... Tina, I only know that if I do want marriage I want it to be with you. I've never met anyone like you before. You sit there. You're tired, you're broke, you have the cares of the world on your shoulders—and I've made you pregnant and I'm leaving for London. But do you dissolve into hysterics? No. Of course not. You sit there and take all the responsibility for our child onto yourself, as you took on the responsibility for your sister and her children.'

'I don't see what use hysterics would be,' Tina said mildly. 'And as for my sister... Christie would have done the same for me.'

'That's just it.' Jock's voice was so intense that Tina blinked. 'She would have done. I know that. Because she loves you as you love her. But not the likes of me. I'd never do that—accept responsibility—because I'm running scared.'

Jock sighed and stood, walking around the desk until he was behind her. His hands came down on Tina's shoulders and he held on, gripping her hard. For a moment—for a long, life-changing moment—Tina let herself lean back against him and feel his strength. She let herself be cradled against him. In that minute she knew that she was lost—that if he said now that he'd stay, she'd hold him to her no matter what the future held, no matter how much against her better judgement it would be.

Jock was her love, she told herself bleakly. She loved him as she could never love another. So... If she could hold him... Take him up on his offer to do what was honourable... Surely in time she could heal the scars? Surely she could teach him what it was to love and be loved in return?

Jock bent and kissed her on the top of her curls, and his eyes were troubled.

'Tina, you must marry me,' he said gently. 'I know... Oh, hell, no, I don't. I don't know anything. But one thing... I do know that I can't walk away. I know I can't go to the other side of the world and leave you to raise our child by yourself. I know I'll have to change, Tina. I'll have to learn to give...learn to love.'

'Jock...'

'No.' He placed a finger on her lips, silencing her. 'Tina, if there's anyone who can possibly do that...teach me to love... If you're willing to take a chance on me then I want you to marry me, and I'll even go down on bended knee to ask you to do it.'

'Oh, Jock...'

How could she refuse this chance? It was only a chance, she knew, a small chance of happiness and an enormous gamble. But what was at stake here? What would she lose if she didn't gamble at all?

'You'll try to love me?' she whispered, and her hand came up to touch his, to feel his strength and his tenderness.

'I'll love you,' Jock said, and if his words were a trifle strained, please, God, she didn't hear it.

If I can, his heart whispered, if I can.

The wedding took place two months later.

As Gundowring weddings went it was small, but by Jock's criteria it was huge. 'We'll invite only our close friends,' he'd said, but everyone in Gundowring thought they were close friends and it was impossible to ask one and not others.

The medical community was out in force. Struan, back from his holidays in high good humour, employed a team of locums from the city for the weekend so no emergency could mar the celebrations. And it was some celebration. The locals *en masse* thought it was just the most romantic wedding they'd ever seen.

Tina... Well, Tina was exquisite. She refused to wear white—though 'everyone does nowadays; it's not as if marrying when you're pregnant is a disgrace any more,' Christie had told her—but she'd compromised by wearing palest gold shantung with white ribands threaded through.

The dress—made by Christie, to whom the wedding had provided a new lease of life and had launched her straight back into bossy big sister mode—was simple and flowing and lovely, fitting Tina's figure to perfection. Christie had allowed room for a tummy bulge but had taken it in at the last minute as there was still no bulge.

Christie was matron of honour, wearing matching gold and looking serene and lovely herself. She'd gained weight and was smiling fit to burst. Ally and Tim were flower girl and page boy respectively, strutting down the aisle proudly as if they'd planned the whole thing.

Christie and her children were right behind this wedding, and they had more reasons than just their fondness for Jock. Jock and Tina had found a farmlet on the out-skirts of town, overlooking the bay. It was truly lovely and its best feature was that it had two houses a couple of hundred yards apart.

'We need you to live near us,' Jock had told Christie. 'Tina wants to keep on working at least part time so we need you—and if you could find it in your heart to need us back, we'd be very grateful.'

Jock always knew the right thing to say, Tina thought to herself as she stood at the entrance to the church. He'd behaved wonderfully all through their engagement. Bought her an engagement ring that had made her gasp, took her out searching for a home, made love to her as if…as if he meant it.

Now he was marrying her. Her beloved Jock was waiting at the end of the aisle, impossibly handsome in his dark suit—impossible for her to refuse. Her Jock. Her love. The first strains of the bridal march trumpeted forth, and Tina stepped forward. Jock turned and smiled, his face alight with love and pride, and Tina would have followed him to the ends of the earth.

Her Jock was waiting. Dear God, she loved him. But if she hadn't loved him so much—if she hadn't known him as she knew herself—she would never have seen the trace of panic still lying behind his eyes and the pervading sense of being trapped.

He loved her, but he didn't want this. As Tina stepped forward to be married she knew that she still had a long way to go before she found true happiness. If she ever did.

CHAPTER TWELVE

IT WASN'T going to work.

It was Tina's last day at the hospital. She stared at her desk in increasing gloom. Five more minutes and then she'd close her drawer, take herself home and face motherhood. Alone. That's what it felt like. Loneliness. Tina had been married to Jock for four months now. In four weeks their baby would be born and they'd be a family, but they couldn't be a family the way Jock was acting.

'Ready to go?' Ellen Silverton walked into the ward, her arms full of bootees. 'Here you are, then. This is the entire production of the women's section of the nursing home for the past month. They're starting on matinée jackets now. If you don't hurry and have this baby, you'll need to have quintuplets to fit all the clothes.'

Tina smiled but her face was strained, and Ellen's sharp eyes noticed.

'Tina, what is it?'

'Nothing.'

'Tell Aunty Ellen.' Ellen perched herself on the opposite chair and frowned. 'Come on, Tina. As of now, you're no longer Dr Rafter to my Sister Silverton. You're an expecting mum on maternity leave, and I have eyes in my head. All's not right with your world.'

'It is.'

'Liar.' Ellen shook her head. 'So what's causing the shadows? Are you worried about the baby?'

'No.' Tina sighed. 'Of course I'm not. I don't have to be—Jock's worried enough for both of us.'

'Now that I don't understand. You've had every test known to man, and your husband's the best obstetrician this place has ever seen. He's organised a locum to back him up during the delivery and the locum's qualifications are almost as good as his. He shouldn't be worried.' Ellen hesitated. 'Or maybe I do understand. His mum was so ill. Maybe it's inevitable that he'll panic.'

'As long as the panic stops,' Tina burst out. 'As long as one day it stops. It's irrational and I can't bear it.'

'You can't bear...'

'He's always watching me as if I'm about to disappear in a puff of smoke.'

'And that worries you?'

'It does.' Tina sat back in her chair and sighed. 'I know. I'm the luckiest woman in the world. I love him so much and he's so good to me. But, Ellen, you don't know what it's like...'

'Is he paranoid?' Ellen asked bluntly.

'Oh, no, nothing so simple. I mean—he's not over the top afraid that something will happen. It's just...it's just that it seems like he expects it. He knows that one day this will end—what's between us—so he doesn't give...'

'What doesn't he give?'

'Himself.' There, she'd said it. Tina bit her lip. She had no business discussing her husband with anyone else, but Christie worshipped the ground Jock walked on and couldn't see past how wonderful he was. Accustomed to a husband who didn't care, Christie thought Jock's caring was magic so Tina couldn't talk to her sister. Whereas Ellen... Ellen had known Jock forever. Maybe she could understand.

'Don't get me wrong,' Tina said slowly. 'He's doing...Jock's doing just the best he knows how. He loves me. He says he does and I believe him. If I didn't believe that I never would have agreed to marry him. I know it's true. And he's kind and gentle and we laugh at the same things and he makes love...' She blushed and managed a faint grin. 'Well, there's no problem in that direction.'

'I'm glad to hear it.'

'But he holds himself...' Tina sighed. 'Heck, Ellen, it's so hard to explain. It's like marriage is his duty, his job—and, by golly, he's going to do it right. When we joke... Like last week, a possum came down the chimney. We thought it was a burglar and Jock armed himself to the teeth with an umbrella and a rolling pin and in he went—into the fray—and all there was was a possum, sitting on the mantelpiece looking silly. Even when we were laughing at three o'clock in the morning at a stupid possum Jock was watching me. As if...he'll enjoy this now, soak this up, because tomorrow...'

'Tomorrow you'll be gone?'

'That's it. Like I'm some lovely bit of porcelain, worth a fortune but with a built-in time bomb and he doesn't know when I'm going to self-destruct.' She grimaced. 'I tell you, Ellen, it puts some strain on things. And when I yell at him—'

'You yell at him?' Ellen asked, startled, and Tina gave a shaky smile, her indestructible sense of humour twinkling out.

'Yeah, I do. Sometimes I do. Don't you sometimes yell at your husband?'

'Well...'

'Oh, come on, Ellen. Like when he does something absolutely unforgivable, like leaving the toilet seat up for the third time in a row, or just because he's being too damned nice and I'm too damned pregnant... Don't you, Ellen?'

'I might,' Ellen said cautiously. 'I'm not saying.'

'And if you might,' Tina went on mercilessly, 'what happens then?'

Ellen stared, and then she blushed. 'He... Bob yells right back,' she admitted. 'Tells me there's too many women in our house and he wants his own toilet. And we get louder and louder, and then we end up with the giggles and often in bed... Though once he emptied a whole packet of frozen peas down my back before he made me laugh and hit the sheets...'

She chuckled in remembrance.

But Tina wasn't smiling. That was what she wanted, she thought, that was what it *could* be like. 'See?'

'But... Isn't that what happens to you?' Ellen probed, and Tina shook her head.

'No way. If I get crabby Jock humours me, as if I'm ill and I'm precious and I'm about to vanish in this puff of smoke—and if he doesn't relax soon I will!'

'Will what?'

Tina jumped, and turned to find Jock, standing in the doorway—white-coated, stethoscope swinging and so handsome he made her heart turn over just as it had the first day she saw him. He was smiling but his eyes were concerned. 'Are you OK, Tina? You sound upset.'

'I'm fine, Jock.' Tina managed a smile but it was a shaky one. 'Ellen was just presenting me with twenty-seven pairs of bootees.' She held a handful for him to inspect. 'Look. So if junior is born with fifty-four feet we're prepared. Any more than fifty-four and we're in trouble.'

He didn't smile. 'Tina, our baby will be perfect,' he said softly, as if to reassure her—as if Tina really was worried about fifty-four feet. He crossed and stooped to give her a swift kiss. 'He'll be perfect, just like his mother. All the tests have told us so. Are you ready to go home now?'

Tina sighed and gave up her attempt at humour. 'Yes. I guess I am. All ready. I'll miss this place.'

'At a guess you won't be away for very long,' Ellen told her, her face troubled as she watched Jock. There was enough in that little interchange for her to see what

Tina was getting at. 'And you have your anaesthetic exams to study for in between nappy changes.'

'There's that.' Tina managed a smile. She pushed herself to her feet. Jock moved to help her and it was all Tina could do not to slap his hand away. 'I'm OK.' She glanced at her watch. She'd gone onto day duty for the last two months and was finishing early. 'It's only five. The shops are still open. I'll do the grocery shopping on the way home, Jock, and I'll see you about seven. Your babies permitting.'

'Mrs Arthur's in labour now but she's slow.' Jock glanced at his watch. 'I should have time. I'll drive you home now and then come back.'

'No,' Tina snapped, but tried to keep her voice civil. 'I'll drive myself home, Jock Blaxton. I'm a perfectly capable adult, you know. Healthy even, believe it or not.'

Tina fretted all the way around the supermarket and half the way to the farm. This was stupid. This was really, really, stupid.

She knew how Jock could be. Relaxed and happy, Jock was the man of her dreams, but he was never relaxed, apart from maybe the times when they were between the sheets and he had her in her arms. There was that, she thought, the sides of her mouth curving into a rueful smile. Maybe they'd just have to spend more time in bed.

Maybe he'd relax more when the baby came, when he knew everything was fine. Maybe. Or maybe he'd worry twice as much.

'Why is everything so complicated?' she demanded of the road ahead. At the edge of town the road twisted upwards into the hills. There were a few scattered farmhouses, the last one on the road being theirs.

'And why am I so miserable?'

It was a gorgeous day. The sun was glittering on the sea and the air was warm and still. She was finishing work to bear the child of her husband, the child of the man she loved. She was protected and cherished and loved...

'So I'm just being selfish,' she muttered. 'I shouldn't want more.'

But she did. She didn't want to be Jock's cherished, protected and beloved wife.

'I want to be his friend, damn it,' she told the road. 'I want to be his lover and his mate. I want to have fun—not be stuck in cotton wool for the rest of my life!'

And then her thoughts ended abruptly. The road moved.

CHAPTER THIRTEEN

FOR a moment Tina thought she was imagining it. Accustomed to her baby doing infantile aerobics inside her, she thought the jolt was just another internal kick. Then it happened again, but this time the steering-wheel jerked under her hands and the car slewed sideways. Tina hit the brakes and stared ahead in stupefaction.

The road was twisting, buckling like an enormous stiff ribbon being turned at each end. Roads don't twist. They don't! Tina's hands gripped the steering-wheel desperately in panic. *They don't!* This one was. The whole world was moving, as if the earth had a giant case of indigestion. A tree ahead tilted at a crazy angle and crashed down across the road, sending a spray of leaves up over her windshield.

Dear God! Tina's breath was coming in frightened gasps. She'd come to a halt on the grass verge at a twenty-degree angle to the horizontal, and the car—and the road—was still moving under her. Should she get out or stay in?

Stay in. Stay in! At least there were no more trees near her and the one in front could fall no further. The bucking went on for ever—or at least two minutes. It was probably the longest two minutes Tina had ever known. With the dramatic twist of the roadway as the tremor started, Tina half expected worse to come—chasms to open, the sky to fall.

'It's an earth tremor,' she told herself, trying desperately to stay calm, to stay rational. 'An earth tremor. Like the one up at Newcastle...'

There had been people killed at Newcastle. The

Newcastle earthquake, just south of Sydney, had been catastrophic.

'This one's out in the open,' Tina told herself. She twisted around to stare out of the car's back window at the town she'd just come from. Gundowring looked placid and peaceful in the sunlight. The sea was calm and still. Nothing had changed.

'So...so it's a localised earth tremor,' Tina whispered. 'It's nothing to be afraid of at all.'

The road wound down to sea level again before home. From here sea level looked good, undamaged. That meant Christie and the kids would be OK. If the only damage was here... But was it? Cautiously Tina climbed from the car, distrusting the solid ground under her feet, expecting it to wobble at any minute.

Nothing happened. Apart from the angle of the road, the crashed tree and the vast crack along the centre of the bitumen, she might well have imagined the whole thing. What now? She couldn't drive on—that was for sure. Apart from anything else, there was a tree blocking her path and the land behind her was more densely wooded than here. If the tremors were still happening she'd be silly to go back that way. She put a hand on her car phone and then hesitated. Telephone? Telephone who?

Jock?

No. No way. He'd come tearing up here like a madman, she told herself. He'd mobilise the fire brigade and the ambulance and the emergency services to rescue his wife, who didn't need rescuing at all. The emergency services could well be needed elsewhere and would waste their time, coming to her aid. She had no guarantee this was just local.

It was only about a mile to the farm. If she walked wide of any tree that looked remotely fallible— Then her thoughts stopped abruptly. Somebody screamed.

Tina hesitated for one second—only one. The scream had held sheer terror and it had been close. She hesitated only long enough to grab her doctor's bag and then started running as fast as her pregnant body would let her.

She didn't get far. A hundred yards from the car—just past the fallen tree—a boy burst from the undergrowth near the road. He was about twelve or so at a guess, in jeans, grubby T-shirt and sneakers. His face was scratched and bleeding, his arm was hanging oddly and his eyes were frantic. He took one look at Tina and headed straight for her—straight into her arms.

Jason Calvert. Town toughy. Tina knew him by sight—and by reputation. He and his mate, Brendan, swaggered round the town acting as though they were sixteen years old. He wasn't sixteen years old now; he was one terrified little boy. Jason grabbed Tina, held her hard—and burst into tears.

'Hey... Jason...'

Somehow Tina managed to pry him loose. She held him at arm's length, not breaking the contact but stooping to meet his eyes. 'Jason. What is it? You've hurt your arm...'

'Oh, miss..' He recognised her then and gave a ragged sob of relief. 'Doc...' He went for the huddle again and she gave in, holding him tightly against her—no mean feat with baby in between. 'Oh, Doc...'

'It's OK, Jason,' she told him. 'It's fine. It was just an earth tremor. Were you hit by the tree? We'll take you down to the hospital and get that arm fixed—'

'No!' He shoved himself away then, fighting for control—fighting back pain and terror. 'No! Miss, it's not me. It's Brendan... Brendan...'

'Where's Brendan?' Tina's voice sharpened. Jason was badly enough hurt, and if he was the one running for help... 'Jason, where is Brendan?'

'We...'

'Calmly,' Tina ordered. 'Three deep breaths first and then tell.'

Finally he did.

'We've...we've been wagging school, like.' Jason gulped. 'There was supposed to be some stupid camp so we told our mums we were going, but then we came up here for the night. Brought some food. We even got some beer...'

Tina knew. Before Jason went on she knew. Why had the boys come here? She'd spent her childhood here so she knew.

'Brendan's in the cave?'

'Yeah. He is. But the whole end... We were just sitting there, trying to get a fire going, and everything shook and roared and the rocks...they just caved in. A rock hit my arm and I ran, but Brendan... When the rocks stopped falling I went back to see... There's a whole heap of stuff lying on his legs and I can't move him.'

Eight months pregnant and on maternity leave, Tina's emergency medical mode still worked on automatic. She clicked straight in, and even Jason's hysteria was checked in the face of her calmness.

'Right. First rule, Jason, and it's the most important one. Don't panic. I need you and you *must* keep a clear head. He's in Bosun's cave?' Bosun's cave was the big one—the one the local kids had labelled a smugglers' cave generations ago. Tina had wagged the odd school day, too.

'Yes... But he's right up the back...'

'I understand, and I know the cave. I'll go there now.'

'I'll show you...'

'No. Your job is to stay here,' Tina said, checking his forward movement. With that damaged arm he was liable to collapse at any minute. She managed a smile. 'I was a school-wagging twerp when I was your age so I know the caves. There's locals that don't, though, so you'll have to bring them when help arrives.'

'But… How…?'

'I want you to go back to my car,' she told him. 'It's not locked. Pick up the mobile phone and dial 000. Rhonda will answer. Tell her calmly—and I mean calmly, Jason, not a tear in sight, mind—everything that's happened. Stay on the line until you've answered every question she has. Then stay in the car until the ambulance comes so you can guide them to us. Wind the driver's seat back so you're lying down and stay there and wait. I'm depending on you, Jason, and so is Brendan. Don't let us down.'

The tremor was felt at the hospital but only as that—a minor tremor. A crack appeared in the plaster in the corridor, a painting crashed in Ward Four and crockery rattled. Mrs Dobson thought she was having a 'turn' and rang her bell in panic.

Waiting between interminable contractions—good grief, this was Mrs Arthur's third baby, you'd think she'd be better at it by now—Jock wandered along to Reception to talk about the tremor—and found semi-organised panic. There were two ambulance officers in the foyer and four men in state emergency gear and…the fire brigade chief?

'What the hell…?' The room off the hospital reception doubled as the region emergency control room. There were men arriving by the minute. Jock turned to Rhonda, the receptionist. 'Rhonda, what's happening?'

'The tremor wasn't as mild as it felt,' Rhonda told him. 'Not up in the hills. So far we've had reports of four houses collapsing—two lots of injuries and there may be more. Telephone lines are down…' Then she hesitated and pointed to the first ambulance. 'Jock, if you

have time... I was going to call Dr Buchanan to see if
she'd go, but if I get her to look after Mrs Arthur instead
you might like to go with Ambulance One. Brendan
Cordy is stuck in a cave up on the ridge. And...'

'And?' By the look on Rhonda's face, Jock knew
there was worse to come.

'Tina's with him,' Rhonda told him. 'She's OK,' she
said hurriedly as she saw his eyes widen, 'but as far as
I know, Tina's in the cave with Brendan.'

The cave entrance was as spooky as Tina had ever seen
it. Only the boldest of kids ever went in here, Tina remembered. Torches were OK near the entrance, but inside their beams were swallowed up by the darkness and
Tina wasn't as brave now as she'd been when she was
twelve. So she stopped at the cave mouth and called.

'Brendan? Can you hear me?'

Maybe if there'd been no reply she'd have waited.
Maybe. But from inside the cave came a faint, pain-filled
moan.

Spooky or not, Tina was in there fast. She carried a
flashlight in her doctor's bag and she paused only long
enough to find it. Then, carefully, mindful of her clum-
siness—heavens, she wasn't as fit as she'd been when
she was twelve, and there was the extra difficulty of the
baby—she walked forward, bending her head so she
wouldn't hit the rocks she remembered being at head
height. Or at shoulder height—heck, she must have
grown.

Then she gave up walking as too dangerous and
started to crawl, ignoring the loose rubble biting into her
knees, holding her torch under her arm and shoving her
bag before her through the dust, until she found him.

Brendan was about fifty yards down into the cave and
his legs were pinned under the rock-fall, but he was con-
scious. His eyes focussed on the beam of light as he

watched her come closer. When she reached the point where she could touch him he gripped her hand, held on as if he were drowning and burst into tears.

'Oh, Doc.. Oh, Doc…'

'You'll be all right, Brendan.' The fact that he'd recognised her and was talking so strongly was a wonderful sign. She flicked the torch beam upwards. The roof here seemed stable enough. If she could just haul away the rocks on his leg…

'Help's on its way,' she told him, feeling more confident by the minute. 'I'll give you something for the pain and then we'll set about getting you out of here.'

And then the earth moved again.

There was one sickening upward jolt. The rocks at the entrance came crashing down, and the world turned to thunder.

'Where did you say this cave was?' Jock's voice was hoarse with fear.

'It's here…' Jason looked wildly around him at the freshly tumbled rocks. 'Somewhere…' But nothing looked familiar any more. Nothing! 'It must be here. I swear. I'm sure the entrance was just by the redgum. But the redgum's fallen…'

'He's right, Doc,' one of the ambulance men said heavily. 'I know this place. This is where the cave entrance used to be.'

Jock stared down with sickening incredulity. There was nothing. No cave. No Brendan. No Tina. Just one vast mound of settling, unstable rocks.

CHAPTER FOURTEEN

Saturday, May 5th
Two missing, feared dead

A young boy, injured and trapped by falling rocks, and the pregnant doctor who went to his aid are today listed as missing after yesterday's earth tremor north of Gundowring. The tremor, measuring 4.1 on the Richter scale, was felt as far north as Bateman's Bay but damage was confined to a small area...

'Oh, God. They must be alive... They must...'

'Jock, let's face it, the chances are slim, to say the least.' Struan's face was nearly as strained as his friend's. 'There must be two hundred tons of earth came down on that cave.'

'They must still be down there... One way or another... Why the hell can't they dig faster?'

'They're digging as fast as they can. The earth's unstable. If they go in fast they risk more rock-falls. And they're flying in electronic sensing equipment from Sydney. If they're alive, we'll find them.'

'When...? But when?'

Sunday, May 6th
Hopes fading for missing pair

Rescuers are conceding the chances of finding anyone alive in the rock-fall north of Gundowring are now exceedingly slim. Sniffer dogs and sophisticated sensing equipment today failed to find any trace...

Monday, May 7th
Despair among rescuers

There is still no sign of life from the rock-fall north of Gundowring. Rescuers are privately admitting that twenty-nine-year-old Dr Tina Rafter, her unborn baby and twelve-year-old Brendan Cordy, the lad she went into the cave to rescue, are probably dead. There are now more than two hundred workers at the site...

'Jock, go home and get some rest.'

'No.'

Christie placed a hand on Jock's shoulder and gripped hard. 'Come on, Jock, This is doing you no good at all. I think it's time we accepted that she's gone—don't you?'

'I...'

'Jock, I'm feeling the same way you are.' There was no denying that. Christie's face was drawn and haggard and she looked as if she hadn't slept for a week. 'But...' She hesitated. 'Jock, we can move on from here. Tina wouldn't want this to destroy us. All I want to know now... All I want to know is that it was quick...'

But Jock was shaking his head.

'There's no moving on,' he said dully.

'Yes, there is.' Christie stared down at him and she saw what was in his heart. She'd been talking to Ellen and she'd seen enough. She wasn't stupid. Jock had expected this. His mother's death had effectively ended his father's life, leaving only bitterness in her place. It mustn't happen to Jock.

So, despite how she was feeling herself—despite the

hopelessness washing over her in waves—Christie had to try. She lifted his hands and pressed them hard.

'Jock, Tina loved you, loved you absolutely. She would have died for you, and that love… It doesn't end with death. We had her for a short while and we were blessed. She lived her life to the full and we loved her for it.'

'Christie, don't…'

'Jock, you have to listen. You must! Jock, if Tina hadn't lived so much maybe she'd be standing here with us today—mourning one little boy who was buried alone. If she hadn't lived so much she wouldn't have taken risks—but, then, she wouldn't have been the Tina we loved. She gave herself, Jock, totally, and that's why we loved her. That's why she'll stay with us.'

'No.' Jock was almost past hearing. He was unshaven and filthy and weary past belief, and he stared at Christie with eyes that hardly registered. He'd dug with his bare hands, desperate, and then, as the digging teams had become organised, he'd dug alongside the miners until he'd been ordered off.

He was in no state to think. But still Christie tried—she had no choice.

'Jock, Tina wasn't a precious thing to be idolised and kept safe. We loved her but now it's time to let her go. Please… For Tina, you have to keep on living. Loving…'

Then Christie's voice faltered. Her voice fell to a whisper and she put her hands to her face. Dear God, she wasn't made of stone. 'Just…just as long as we know that it was quick!' she whispered. 'Please, God…'

Her voice was laced with despair, and Jock was shaken enough to look swiftly at her. For the first time he saw past his own misery. He saw Christie's total exhaustion, and he saw the love that made her reach out, past her own despair, to try and help him.

Tina was right, he thought slowly, wondering. Life did go on, and he knew then what Tina would want him to do. It was as Christie had said. His father had let his mother's death destroy his life, destroy his son's life, but Tina... Tina would want him to live on, to love as he'd never been able to live and to love before—even when he'd had his Tina at his side.

Suddenly he saw the gift Tina had given him, and it was like the lifting of a black, cold fog, letting in the light that had been outside all along. Dear God, that Tina could only live to know...

'Come on, Christie,' he said softly, and he rose stiffly from the log where he'd been sitting for hours. Days. 'I'll take you home. And then I'll come back here and wait some more. But, Christie...' He shook his head, as though trying to shake off a nightmare. 'Maybe you're right,' he managed. 'Whatever happens... Maybe we can still let her live.'

Monday 7th—Evening Extra
ALIVE?

Sensitive electronic probes today detected signs of life deep under the ground in the rubble from the Gundowring quake. Rescuers are cautious of raising hopes at this stage, but manpower on the site has been increased. It is believed that three hundred men will be digging through the night...

Jock was the first to see her. There had been pressure on him to stay back—pressure because they were unsure of what they would find. But then there had been a voice—husky at first and incredulous, as if the thought that someone could hear her could be nothing but a dream. Tina. After three days buried, unbelievably it was Tina.

The probe picked up her calls as faint echoes and then, almost not daring to breathe, the technicians adjusted the probe, moved it and adjusted it again. They heard words, faint but true.

'I'm OK. I'm hungry as a horse, my legs are so stiff I can hardly move—even if there was room—and I'm so thirsty that my tongue's swollen, but Brendan and I are fine.'

'Brendan?' Beside Jock, Brendan's parents were close to collapse.

'Brendan's broken his leg.' Tina's voice cracked with dryness. 'It took us a while to get him clear of the fall, but the leg should be OK. He still has circulation. We're in a crevice about five feet square, and Brendan wants his mum and a can of Coke like nothing else on earth, but we're OK.'

'And what do you want?' The captain of the State Emergency Service was grinning like a Cheshire cat. This was an ending everyone had ceased even to hope for. 'What do you want, Dr Rafter?'

There was silence, and then the voice fell to a shaky whisper.

'Please, God... Please, God, I just want my Jock.'

'Hold on there, Tina. He's on his way.'

It couldn't be that easy—and it wasn't. It took five more hours of digging and all the skill in the world—they didn't need another rock slip at this stage—to reach them.

Then Jock was allowed over the pile of rocks—down through the shored-up tunnel which had taken so much manpower to build—and he was there, squeezed in with the miners, when the final rock between them was moved... And there was Tina. She was battered and filthy, but she was unbelievably alive in the torchlight— and, unbelievingly, she was managing to smile.

'Jock,' she whispered, and her hand came through the gap and gripped with a strength he wouldn't have believed possible. She held on as if she were drowning.

'We'll get you out,' Jock managed, his voice breaking with emotion. 'Oh, Tina..'

'That'd be appreciated,' she said hoarsely. 'And…and make it fast. Because…Jock, I have the most dreadful back pains…'

'Back pains.' Visions of a fractured spine flooded through him, and the tension in the group of miners increased to breaking point. Jock could feel the men around him tense. 'Hell, Tina, don't try and move. We'll get you out flat on a stretcher…'

'I'm waiting for no stretcher,' Tina told him, her voice strengthening. 'No way. You just get this hole a bit bigger—a lot bigger—and I'm coming out anyway I can because, Jock…'

'Tina?'

'I'm coming out and so…' She gave a ragged gasp of fear. 'Oh, Jock, so's our baby, and I don't think Brendan fancies himself as a midwife.'

Jessica Christine Blaxton was born at three a.m. in the morning at the mouth of the most makeshift tunnel Jock had ever seen—and if Struan Maitland as doctor in charge hadn't ordered screens to be placed around the cave entrance the world press would have watched the birth.

There was no time to get Tina to hospital. As Christie said laughingly about it later, there had been no time for anything.

'You're a paddock breeder, my dear,' she said. 'A month premature with your first baby and there was barely time to catch her.'

But Jock had caught her. He stood in the still night

air while rescuers cheered and wept and hugged each other around him and he knew... In that one crystalline moment, which would stay with him for ever, Jock Blaxton knew that he was truly blessed.

CHAPTER FIFTEEN

'ARE you ready to come home, Mrs Blaxton?'

Tina stretched out in her hospital bed like a cat, moving every one of her limbs in turn. Even two weeks after being released from her underground prison it still felt unbelievably good to move.

'Convince me.' Tina smiled happily up at her husband. 'In hospital I have menus for every meal, nurses to change Jessie's nappy, my friends around me and you seemingly on tap. What does home have to offer that this place doesn't?'

Jock's eyes glinted. He bent and kissed his wife on the lips—a long, toe-curling kiss that had her heart doing handstands.

'How about a double bed?' he whispered.

Tina's delicious chuckle rang out through the ward.

'Sold. I'm convinced. Grab the baggage and the baby. Take me home immediately. Or on second thoughts...'

Her own eyes twinkled. Tina's arms wrapped themselves around her husband and she hauled him backwards onto the bed. 'Can I wait that long? A single bed is fine...'

'Not with a glass insert in the door it's not,' Jock retorted. But he wasn't completely refusing. Regardless of passing nurses, he held her close and let his long body relax on the bed, moulding her lovely body against his. 'Hell, Tina...' His smile died.

'No.' She placed her finger on his lips. 'No, Jock. Don't think about it.'

He shook his head and his hold tightened. 'I just can't believe that I have you back.'

The whole world was still marvelling about their escape. Apart from healing cuts and fading bruises, Tina was fine. Brendan was recovering as well. He was trussed up in traction in the children's ward, sitting up in bed to boast of his exploits to all and sundry. But holding his parents' hands—hard. There were still scars, Jock knew, and he knew, when Tina held him close, that she couldn't shrug everything off.

They'd been so lucky. Lucky that the roof had held, that one huge slab of granite had fallen right in front of them and they'd been protected. Lucky that so many people had been prepared to work around the clock against seemingly hopeless odds.

And lucky that Tina had had her doctor's bag, with antibiotics, intravenous saline and morphine to keep Brendan's pain and dehydration and infection at bay. She'd held Brendan and comforted him and had told him over and over that they'd be rescued—and she'd been right.

Eventually.

Jock felt himself shudder and he looked up to find Tina watching him, her face troubled.

'What is, love?' he asked.

'Jock…' Tina hesitated. 'I know… I know this is silly, but…'

'But what?'

'How are you going to keep me safe from earthquakes?'

Jock's face stilled.

'Tina…'

'You were frantic about me before,' she whispered. 'What now?' Then she moved to look down into the crib beside the bed. Jessica Christine Blaxton was almost due for a feed and was starting to stir. 'Will you let us…?'

'Let you what?'

'Let us be…us?'

Silence.

Jock closed his eyes. He held his wife in his arms and let his fingers run though her fiery curls—and he knew what she was asking.

'Tina—'

'Jock, you never wanted us,' Tina burst out. 'All the time I was trapped I kept thinking...this...this awfulness is just what you expected. This is what you were most afraid of, and I've done it to you. You didn't want to love me, Jock, you didn't want a family. I've caused you such pain, and I'm so sorry.'

'Don't!'

Jock straightened on the bed, and his eyes blazed. He held Tina at arm's length and anger surged through him. 'Don't, Tina. Don't you ever dare be sorry. Not ever.'

'But—'

'I said no! No way! Because you're apologising for being you,' he told her roughly, and he pulled her into his arms again, holding her in a grip of iron. 'Tina, it's me who's been so unfair. It's me who hasn't seen straight. Christie said it. When you were down that hole and we thought you were dead. And I'd been so blind...'

'What...?'

'Christie said that you give yourself. She said that's why we love you and that's why you'll stay with us, dead or not. You'll always be with us.

'Tina, I've been a fool,' he said softly. 'A blind, stupid fool. I've almost destroyed the thing I hold most precious in the world. Christie's right, Tina. I can never lose you—you're part of me.' He put his mouth against hers and he kissed her. 'You're part of my life, you've made me whole again and one day... God forbid but one day if death divides us then that part will still be with me.'

He kissed her again, tenderly, gently, and there was wonder in his voice.

'I want eighty years of married life with you, my love. My heart. Or more if I can wangle it. And I'll keep on protecting you and our little Jessie, but not because I'm terrified of losing you. Not that. Because I know now that I can't lose you. You're a part of me, and because of you I'm a different person. For ever.'

'Jock...'

'Tina, I'll protect you and cherish you because I love you,' he said softly, holding her close to him, close to his heart. 'And we'll have fun, my lovely Tina. We'll enjoy life to the full.' He shook his head, his eyes firm and sure, telling her that he spoke the truth.

'My love's changed,' he told her. 'For ever. From now on... From now on you'll be my wife and my lover and my friend. I want you to marry me, Tina. Not like before. Properly. For ever. Please, Tina...'

All of a sudden his eyes were anxious as if, even now, she could say that it wasn't on, that it was too late, that he'd killed her love.

But nothing could kill her love. Nothing.

Jessica stirred and whimpered in the cot beside the bed, and Jock released Tina long enough to lift his daughter and place her in Tina's arms. Then he held them both. And Tina held her tiny daughter close and thought her heart would burst.

'But... what about our little Jessie?' she said softly, her eyes not leaving her husband. Her eyes loving him, loving her family, and her heart full of wonder. 'Is there still one baby too many in the world, Jock? Is our Jessie one baby too many?'

'No way.' Jock pulled his wife and child closer into his arms and held them as if he'd never let them go. 'Did I ever say there was one baby too many in the world? I must have been mad.'

He looked down at his wife and his infant daughter and his face told Tina all she would ever want to know.